Whiskey & Wine

REBECCA GANNON

Rebecca Gannon

Website, blog, shop, and links to all social media:
www.rebeccagannon.com

More by Rebecca Gannon

Pine Cove
Her Maine Attraction
Her Maine Reaction
Her Maine Risk
Her Maine Distraction

Carfano Crime Family
Casino King
The Boss
Vengeance
Executioner

Standalone Novels
Whiskey & Wine

To everyone who sees the magic in the cold and snowy days of winter,
this is for you.

Author's Note

A very special thank you to the entirety of the Niagara-on-the-Lake Icewine Festival in Ontario, Canada. I stumbled upon the festival's site randomly and knew I needed to go to it despite never having tried icewine. And it was so fun! Especially in a blizzard! I wrote down so many scenes to include that weekend, and I hope I did the festival justice!

Another special thank you to Wayne Gretzky Estates – the inspiration behind Breaker Estates. I the moment I set foot there, I had this book idea hit me like a freight train, and three years later, here it is!

AND to Peller Estates – the inspiration behind the icewine marshmallows! I had so much fun out in the snow around your fire pits, trying not to freeze!

If you're reading this before January 2023 and this book makes you want to go to the next festival, then I'll see you there!

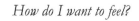

How do I want to feel?

I want to be adored
and I want to feel safe.
I want someone who feels
our hearts were forged the same.

-Mirtha Michelle Castro Mármol

Chapter 1

Lifting my face to the light flakes falling, I close my eyes and breathe them in, my lungs filling with the magic that snow always brings. I blink my eyes open again and look around at the dusting of white beginning to cover everything in sight, a small smile spreading across my face.

Snow and I are old friends.

I was always the first one outside on snow days as a kid, ready to play until my fingers were numb and my hair was frozen into icicles while my mom yelled at me to get inside before I became one. She would shake her head and smile at me as she did so, knowing I was happy to play all day.

Toronto is so beautiful when it's blanketed in snow.

Growing up in upstate New York, I'm used to it, but I'll never grow tired of it.

Inhaling one more deep breath of snowy air, I walk through the doors of the office building where I work and head straight for the elevators. When the doors slide open on the fifth floor, I step out and smile at the urns on either side of the frosted glass doors of Violet's Event Designs and Planning. The urns are overflowing with a wintry blend of flowers, consisting of balsam branches, red berries, snow flocked pinecones, and a mix of white and off-white flowers, bringing the feelings of winter inside.

Shedding my hat, scarf, gloves, and coat, I place each piece on their own hook on my coat rack in my office to dry and settle into the white leather chair behind my desk. But before I can even log into my computer, my phone rings, the red light blinking next to my boss's name.

I smile to myself. "Good morning, Violet."

"Come to my office straight away," she says, and then hangs up, her voice laced with panic. Oh no, this can't be good.

She should be in a good mood after we just finished our biggest wedding of the year, but I guess there's another fire to put out. It was a New Year's Eve wedding that had a limitless budget for some big Financial CEO's daughter and her millionaire fiancé. It was crazy, but I have to say, despite the days I wanted to cry at how demanding and particular the bride and her mother were, I powered through and gave them a damn good wedding I'm proud of.

Violet of Violet's Event Designs is my aunt, but I've

earned my place in her company. I have an Associate's degree in business and marketing, along with completing disciplined courses in Event and Wedding Planning, and Floral and Interior Design from the New York Institute of Art and Design.

Aunt Violet was the family member I always looked up to and wanted to be just like. I lived and interned with her every summer up here in Toronto since I was a sophomore in high school, begging her to take me everywhere she went and to let me help in any way I could. She saw the passion in my persistence.

I love my job, and I make sure I work harder than everyone else so they know I wasn't handed my job at the most competitive, desired, and well-known event company in the city simply because I'm related to the owner.

"Good morning, Violet," I greet, walking into her office two doors down from mine. She's demanded since I was sixteen that I never call her Aunt Violet while working for her, wanting me to know I wasn't her niece during that time. I was her employee and there to learn and work.

She huffs out a breath and motions to the chair in front of her desk. "Leah, please sit. We have a lot to discuss."

"Is something wrong?"

"Yes. Janet has to come back straight away to care for her mother, and the Icewine Festival begins at the end of the week."

"Is her mother alright?"

"She should be, but she needs help, and Janet is the only family she has left." A look crosses my aunt's face, and I know she's probably thinking about her own loneliness. I'm her only family here in Canada. But as quickly as the look crossed her face, it's gone. "Now, Janet has been coordinating and running this festival for Breaker Estates for the past eight years. She has mostly everything in place, but we still need someone to finish all the details and be there to run the three weekends of the festival."

"Okay, what do you need from me?"

"I need you to be that someone. I need you to go there and take over."

"Really?" Excitement courses through me at the opportunity to take on such a big account. Most events we deal with are just one day, or sometimes a weekend affair if we're handling the rehearsal dinner, wedding, and brunch the next day. But three weeks? That's something else entirely.

"Yes, really. I know you just finished with the Callahan wedding this weekend and it was draining, but I need you there. I trust you to take over, Leah. I know you'll make this event shine for the company. But more importantly, for the client."

"Of course." I smile brightly. "It's sad how it's come to me, but I promise I'll do you proud."

"I know you will."

"Can I ask why we take on this event? Don't they have an in-house event manager?"

"No, they don't," she says. "They're marketed as a venue only, so the only part they deal with is the booking. Everything else is up to the person hosting the event or their planner."

"That's odd. They could get so much more business if they had an event coordinator."

"I know. Trust me, I've been bothered by it for years." She shakes her head. "But that's not my problem. Now, you better get going so you can pack and head out today. The events you've been working on that will be happening while you're away will be divided between those here, but everything else you can still work on between everything, yes?"

"Of course," I assure her.

"Good. I'll have all the information for your accommodations, schedule, notes, and plans from Janet forwarded to you straight away."

"Sounds good." I nod, standing.

"You know who owns Breaker Estates, don't you?" she asks as an afterthought.

"No. I was going to research it all tonight when I get there."

"Ben Breaker." When she sees zero recognition on my face, she sighs. "He was a professional hockey player who bought his parent's winery when he retired. Make sure you do your homework so you know what you're walking into."

"I will. You know I'm always thorough."

"I know. Now, head off so you can make it there before dark."

Back in my office, I grab my things and head back out into the snow, a smile stretching across my face. I'm so freaking excited! I've never been to Niagara-on-the-Lake, and I love wine, so I hope I get to tour a few wineries over the next few weeks.

※ ※ ※ ※

I'm staying at a cute inn in town, and because I had to pack almost a month's worth of winter clothes, I end up taking three trips before all of my bags are inside. Toronto is less than two hours away, but I don't know if I'll be able to make it back at all between the festival weekends.

Speaking of which, I climb up on the bed with my laptop and open the documents sent to me from both Janet and Violet, pushing all overwhelming feelings of doing this on my own out of my mind.

I've got this.

First, I familiarize myself with the festival itself. Every Friday, Saturday, and Sunday of the three weekends will have a myriad of events. Opening night, on January 7th, there will be a gala at the Niagara Falls Resort and Casino, and will close on the 23rd with an afterparty at one of the wineries.

There are 29 wineries participating this year, and each one will pair whichever icewine they want featured with a small food that has icewine as one of its ingredients. Those attending the festival can purchase a pass that's good for six food and icewine pairings over the course of their chosen weekend. It's like bar hopping, where you go from winery to winery until your pass is full, with the opportunity to buy another if you'd like. There's even a designated driver's pass that's discounted and for food only.

Reading the list, my mouth begins to water at all of the

choices. There's fried chicken and waffles with an icewine syrup, an icewine glazed bacon quiche puff pastry, a spicy icewine jambalaya, an icewine poached pear over homemade vanilla ice cream, and even icewine glazed meatballs in a homemade sauce.

For those not wanting to travel between the wineries, Main Street in the center of town will be blocked off for the last two weekends where a select group of wineries will have their own booths set up for a mini wine and food tasting all in one spot. Then, one of the nights, the area will be used for a cocktail making competition with live music.

There will also be an icewine brunch hosted by one of the wineries and a dinner at another, where wines and icewines from the area will be available to taste and will be paired with each dish.

At Breaker Estates, I see they're pairing their award-winning Vidal Icewine with a lobster bisque.

Huh.

An icewine lobster bisque? That goes together?

I add that to my ever-growing list of notes and questions I've been compiling, making sure I have the chance to taste the pairing before opening day this weekend.

I know how much work Janet has put into this, but it seems she's done the same thing for the past five years – since Ben Breaker has taken over the winery. He's made a lot of changes to the property and business, like adding the distillery and restaurant, but he hasn't changed their impact and involvement in the festival.

That might have to change.

I don't do things half-way. I have the chance to make an impression and prove myself, and I plan to do just that.

The only problem in that might be the fact that Ben's a hockey legend and arguably the most good-looking man I've ever seen. The internet search I did on him gave more than enough images of him on and off the ice, and clothed and half-clothed, to star in my fantasies for years to come.

I don't want to dig too much into him, because I'm a firm believer that the internet is a breeding ground for nothing but rumors, hearsay, and straight-up lies where athletes and celebrities are concerned.

But...

I can't help seeing the tabloid articles centering around a tell-all from his then girlfriend about how he was a womanizing cheater who treated her like a servant, demanding she cook and clean for him in a maid's uniform and call him sir like he was her boss. And not in a kinky or hot way. It also says he used to bring other women home after any fight they'd have to revenge fuck them in front of her to show that he could have anyone he wants.

Whoa. Wait.

What the hell?

No, this can't be true.

That would make him the biggest douchebag around. And I'll be working with him for the next three weeks...

Great.

Clicking out of that article, I move on to the actual sports ones. He was known as Ben 'The Bone' Breaker. He was drafted to the Rangers straight after graduating from the

University of Wisconsin and was their enforcer for three years before being traded to the Maple Leafs. He then played with them for seven years until he retired after an injury. That's when he bought his parent's winery.

The only sports I follow are baseball and football, so I have to do another search on what an enforcer is/does.

Oh…

Why do I find that incredibly hot that he was the one defending his teammates and getting into fights? Probably because I'm imagining him defending me like that for someone talking shit or hitting on me. And while it's barbaric, it's still sexy.

Okay, it seems my imagination is getting ahead of me. I just hope when I meet him tomorrow, I can look past his hotness and act normal. I need to be professional. I need to make sure he knows I'm not someone who will be intimidated or starstruck by who he is or how he looks.

Considering I didn't know who he was before tonight, I think I'll be fine.

I hope I'll be fine.

Chapter 2

Waking up early, I shower, curl my hair, and do my makeup before digging through my suitcases to find the perfect outfit to make a good impression. I decide to go with a light grey oversized sweater dress, and pair it with tights and over-the-knee heeled black boots.

Tossing my favorite black scarf around my neck that has soft furry pompoms at the bottom, I shrug on my black peacoat and slip my notebook and laptop into my bag.

I passed out last night without having any dinner and now my stomach is growling like a bear, ready to attack me if I don't feed it.

I didn't make it to the inn yesterday before nightfall, so seeing the town in the morning light is something else.

Everything is covered in snow, and I squint as I look around, the sun glistening off the top layer like a million sparkling diamonds.

As I pass a café, I sigh in relief and pull into the parking lot, desperately in need of caffeine and breakfast.

The scent of strong coffee greets me when I walk through the doors and I almost groan. Thank God I hold it in though, because the place has five or six people milling about that would certainly think I was a crazy person if I did.

"Good morning, what can I get for you?" A young girl asks me from behind the counter.

"Hi." I smile. "I'll have a large coffee and…"–I quickly scan the menu written on the wall behind her–"an egg and cheese sandwich on a toasted croissant. Thank you."

"No problem. Can I have a name for the order?"

"Leah."

"Great, thanks. I'll call you when it's ready."

Smiling my thanks, I sit at an empty table and take out my notebook with my agenda for the day. I need to find Ben and introduce myself straight away, then sit with him to go over everything he and Janet have discussed. She sent me as much, but I want to hear everything for myself so I know we're on the same page.

When my name is called, I shove my phone and notebook in my bag and stand. I'm not paying attention though, and as I shoulder my bag, it swings out and hits someone walking by.

"Oh, I'm so sorry!" I turn and say in a rush, just as hot coffee splashes down the front of my dress and all over the floor. Gasping, I jump back and swipe the coffee away with my hand as best as I can before it sets in. "Ow. Damn it," I grind out, burning my hands on the coffee.

"Here," a deep voice says, and a pile of napkins comes into my line of sight.

"Thanks," I mumble, still looking down at my dress. "I hope it doesn't stain. I don't have time to change before–" I cut myself off, realizing I'm babbling and giving way too much information to a stranger. "Never mind. It was my fault. Please, let me buy you a new cup," I offer, my eyes finally looking up at who I bumped into.

Oh.

Holy shit.

It's him.

He's even more gorgeous in person, and I feel my cheeks heat immediately from embarrassment.

Ben Breaker.

He's tall, at least 6'4", with a face that would most definitely win People's next Sexiness Man Alive issue. He was a little bit of a pretty-boy charmer in all those pictures I saw of him, but now he's rugged, sexy, and *all* man.

His light brown hair is on the longer side that I can tell he runs his hands through, his square jaw is cut into hard angles and covered in a light scruff, and his strong brow line gives way to a pair of dark blue eyes the color of the sky when morphing from twilight to night. I want to look into them longer, but with the way he's currently staring at me, I dart mine away, hoping he doesn't see my reaction to him.

"Uh, what did you have?" I ask pointing at his cup.

"Coffee. Black." Those two simple words pierce through me, his deep voice sliced with annoyance.

"I'll buy you a new cup," I tell him in a rush as he grabs a stack of napkins from the station behind him and squats down to swipe the coffee from the floor.

Taking a step back, I clear my throat, trying not to sound tongue-tied when I ask, "You're Ben Breaker, right?"

His eyes snap up to mine from his lower position. "Yes," he clips, standing.

I give him a friendly smile, wanting to give him a better first impression of me. "I'm Leah, and I'm—"

"It's always nice to meet a fan, but I need to go. Don't worry about the coffee."

Taken aback, I don't have time to respond before he's out the door and I'm left standing there like an idiot. He didn't even let me finish. If I really was a fan trying to say hi, he was rude and cold. Is this how he is with everyone? How has he been so successful in business when he clearly lacks decent basic social skills?

I guess our meeting later will be another awkward encounter.

The girl behind the counter calls my name for my order again, and deciding not to risk any more accidents, I sit back down and eat my breakfast sandwich here instead of on the way.

Pulling into the lot of Breaker Estates, my eyes widen. It's gorgeous. Modern, with a sleek steel frame and wooden siding, and yet still manages to bleed a warm and inviting feeling with lots of tall windows – a great contrast to the owner.

Entering through the front doors, I walk up a ramp that has pictures lining the walls of the winery and the Breaker family through the decades on either side of me. I stop and study the ones I see of Ben as a kid, picking grapes from the vines in the fall and running through the snowy vines in the winter. I can't help but smile at the carefree grin he's giving the camera.

When I make it to the top, I turn to the left and am greeted with a view of the entire estate and beyond through a wall of floor-to-ceiling windows.

From Janet's notes and pictures, I know this is the wine tasting room, and where the food and icewine pairings will take place during the festival. It's definitely large enough to hold over a hundred people at once, with lounge styled seating and tables throughout.

Walking up to the windows, I look out at the ice rink below. The building is in a squared off 'u' shape, and the rink sits between the two longer sides of the building like a centerpiece.

Covered in frost and snow, I find it hard to believe this place could be any more beautiful than it is now.

Wanting a closer look, I push out the glass door and descend the large spiral staircase that leads to a slate grey flagstone patio, my boots crunching under the salt and snow. I take a deep breath, my lungs filling with the cold late-morning air. There are a few people already skating out on the rink and I take a seat on a bench to sip my coffee and watch for a minute.

I always do this when I go to a new venue I'm working with. I like to soak it all in so that I can bring the client the best of what their event can be. Especially when I do corporate events and parties where I'm given carte blanche to come up with themes and décor that will paint the company in the best light to whomever they're trying to impress.

Even when a bride has a specific vision as to what her day should look like, I still make sure the space represents that in my own way. Event design and planning is more than just setting a table with a centerpiece while waiting for people to show up. It's creating an entire atmosphere. It's making sure the moment someone steps into the room, they know their night will be well spent and not wish they were at home instead.

It's the subtle details that make the most impact. It's anticipating the needs of the client and then executing it all while making it look easy, when in fact a million little things went into the final product, and a million little things went wrong leading up to the last second before the doors were opened. It always comes together in the end, though.

"Can I help you?" someone asks, and I'm shaken from my own thoughts.

A man who seems to be in his late forties with salt and pepper hair, warm brown eyes, and a soft smile, is standing a few feet away. "I'm just taking it all in," I tell him. "Do you work here?"

"Yes, ma'am. I'm Charlie, the master distiller."

"Oh." I smile. "Do you know where I can find Ben Breaker?" I see the apprehension in his eyes, but I stand and hold my hand out for him. "I'm Leah from Violet's Event Designs and Planning. I'm taking over for Janet."

His apprehension is replaced by a wide grin as he shakes my hand. "Good to meet you, Leah. I'll take you to his office."

"Thank you."

Leading me around the rink, I toss my coffee cup in the trash before we go inside The Whiskey Room entrance, which is the restaurant and bar attached to the distillery. Taking me around the side of the bar and down a short hallway, we go up a set of stairs that overlooks the distillery stills where there's a single door at the end of the landing, marked 'private'.

I take a deep breath and prepare myself for my second introduction to Ben. I hope this one goes a little smoother.

Charlie knocks twice. "Hey, Ben. I've got Janet's replacement here."

"Come in," we hear him say, and Charlie swings the door open wide for me. I step inside, my eyes taking in Ben behind his desk, a determined look on his face.

He continues to stare at his computer screen, but when he finally looks up and his eyes lock with mine, surprise flashes through them. "*You're* taking over for Janet?" he asks incredulously.

"Yes." I nod. "I tried introducing myself earlier this morning, but…" I trail off, giving him a small smile.

His eyes roam over me. "How old are you?" he asks, as if I look like a teen intern or something. "Do you have any experience running an event like this?"

All the warm and fuzzy feelings I may have been feeling towards him vanish in the blink of an eye at his questioning of my abilities.

"I'll just leave you two to discuss this privately," Charlie mutters, backing out and closing the door.

I take a breath before I respond. "If you must know, I'm 27, and yes, I do have more than enough experience to handle this. I was personally asked above everyone else at the company to take over. Violet trusts me to get the job done, *and* do it well beyond your expectations."

I'm usually calm and collected, and friendly to a fault to everyone I meet, but there's something about this man that's making me feel defensive and off my game, and I don't like it.

Rubbing his jaw, he releases a long breath. "Alright. Have a seat."

Thanks for the permission, I say to myself, sitting in the chair across from him. "I've already familiarized myself with and gone over everything Janet sent me in regards to your winery's part in the festival, but I have some questions."

"And they are?"

"I see you've made great improvements and expansions since you've taken over, but you haven't capitalized on them for the festival."

"What do you mean?" he asks, a bite in his tone.

"You do the bare minimum when it comes to showcasing this place. Why haven't you hosted one of the events or come up with one of your own to add to the list?"

"Because I don't like the attention."

I hold back a laugh. "Seriously?"

"Yes," he says through a clenched jaw. "We've done it for years the way it is and there hasn't been a problem. You don't know anything about this place, me, or the event. We're only four days from opening day. Just stick with what Janet has done and try not to mess this up."

Shocked, I clamp my jaw together to keep from having it hang open at his audacity.

Standing abruptly, I walk to the door, but turn back to face him. "You don't know me either, but I put my everything into every job I take on. Just because I've never worked something like this doesn't mean I don't know what I'm doing. If you don't want to increase business or show this place off to as many people as possible, that's your prerogative. I only had a few ideas I thought I'd share. Now, if you'll excuse me, I'm going to go find the chef so I can taste the food and wine pairing for myself."

I pull the door open and storm out of there, anger I'm not used to burning through me. I don't know who Ben Breaker thinks he is, but he's pushing *all* of my buttons in the short span of an hour.

Huffing out a long breath, I descend the stairs and weave my way around the distillery, finding Charlie again.

"Do you think you could show me to the kitchen? I want to meet the chef."

"Sure. Follow me." He must read the residual look on my face from my second interaction with Ben today, because he tells me gently, "You have to give him a chance. He's not big on change."

"The first thing he did when he took over this place was make some very big changes."

"True. But that was him doing the work behind the scenes. When it comes to anything involving publicity and events…" he trails off, trying to find the right words. "He can be difficult."

"You can say that again," I mutter, but then stupidly realize that his aversion to publicity probably stems from everything I read online last night. His personal life was eviscerated by the press and he had so many things said about him, I can't really blame him for wanting to hide. But it's been five years. Surely people have pushed all of that to the backs of their minds or forgotten about it completely.

Charlie pushes open the swinging kitchen doors. "Oh, hey Kate, this is Leah. She's taking over for Janet. Leah, this is Kate, our head wine maker. She's been here a lot longer than I have and has known Ben since he was a teenager. So, she's seen it all with him."

"Don't make me sound so old," she berates, giving him a stern look, then smiles at me. "It's nice to meet you, Leah."

I smile brightly. "It's nice to meet you, too."

"Let me know if you need anything from me or have any questions. You can find me in the barrel room."

"The barrel room?"

"It's beneath the tasting room. We host events down there in one section, but I work in the back, where the magic happens."

"Good to know. Thanks."

Charlie guides me further into the kitchen and right up

to a man dressed in all white. "Alright, here we are. Chef Casey, this is Leah. She's taking over for Janet."

"Hi, Chef. It's good to meet you."

"You, too." Chef Casey is a lot younger than I would've expected, maybe in his late thirties, and handsome in a way that makes a girl wish she could wake up to him cooking her breakfast in an apron and nothing else. Which means he's *very* handsome.

Pushing those thoughts away, I clear my throat. "I was wondering if you had any of the lobster bisque you plan on serving so I can have my own tasting before the weekend?"

"I can make a small batch and have it ready for you tomorrow."

"Perfect." I beam. "Thank you so much."

His warm brown eyes melt a little. "No problem. If you want coffee or tea or anything, help yourself over there at the server's station." He nods to the area to the right, his hands busy whisking something in a bowl.

"Thanks." Walking over, I pour myself a cup of coffee and sip it black, loving the jolt to my senses before adding a little cream and sugar. Charlie is out by the bar when I leave the kitchen, and I give him a little wave as I head back outside and up the spiral stairs to the main tasting room. Taking a seat at the bar so I have a view of the room and the windows to the outside, I pull out my laptop and open up the floor plan Janet sent me, looking around to see it for myself.

It'll work.

Everything Janet has planned will work. I just want to put my own stamp on it somehow. I'm not someone who just does something to get it done.

Sighing, I email all the vendors and people involved in the festival to inform them I'll be taking over and to contact me with any problems or questions from here on out.

When I finally come up for air, I see that a few hours have gone by and I'm starving. Standing, I stretch my neck out and shove my laptop back in my bag. Ben may not want to add events, but that won't stop me from turning this place into a winter haven for everyone who makes Breaker Estates a stop on their weekend tour. I just hate that I know I have to face him again and ask permission to do so, though.

✳ ✳ ✳ ✳

Knocking on Ben's office door when I get back from lunch, I take a deep breath, preparing myself.

"Come in," I hear him rumble through the closed door, and my heart picks up in speed. I hate that he can get a reaction out of me despite the fact that he's rude and surly. I'm here to do my job.

Stepping inside his office, I clear my throat, making him look up. His eyes roam over my face, probably trying to gauge my mood, and then they find mine, those two deep blue pools holding me in place by the door.

Blinking out of the trance, I clear my throat and take the seat in front of him again.

"I realize this morning we didn't get off on the right foot, but I'm here to hopefully change that. I know you don't want to change anything or add any events, and I understand that since the event is so close, but I did have just a few small things I wanted to run by you that won't be a hinderance to you at all."

He gives me a tight nod and I pull out my notebook to show him the rough sketches I made this afternoon.

"I was thinking we could string up white lights that go from different points on the roof to the ice rink. It'll create such a pretty winter wonderland effect and have people still wanting to go outside even when the sun sets." I look up from my notebook to find him staring at me and not my sketch. "What do you think?"

"It's fine. You can go ahead with it."

"Really?" I give him a big smile and then flip to the next page. "I was also thinking that maybe we can put some fire pits outside to have going throughout the day. That way people will want to go outside and stick around after the tasting to enjoy the property, watch people skate, and order another glass of something."

"I like that idea, too. I've been meaning to look into that."

"Hmm," I hum just a little bit haughtily, the corner of my mouth tilting up in the smallest of grins. "I'll get on that right away then since we only have a few days." Closing my notebook, I place it back in my bag.

"Leah."

My heart stops momentarily.

I've never heard my name said in such a husky way before. It makes me think of him saying it while he has me pushed up against his office wall, his breath hot against my skin and—

Whoa.

Okay.

I need to calm down or I'm more than certain he'll be able to tell where my mind has gone by the reddening of my cheeks.

Brushing my hair over my shoulders, I tuck it behind my ears and then look him in the eyes again.

"I'm sorry for earlier," he says.

I'm caught off guard by the sincerity of his words and moment of kindness, but I shake it off and give him a small smile. "Thank you for that. I appreciate it. I didn't mean to come in here and change everything you're used to. I just wanted to share some ideas I had."

"I like what we've been doing and I don't need anything more. But I do think the lights and fire pits are something we should incorporate."

"Good." I smile wide. "I'll go make the calls and have everything delivered in the next couple of days so it can be set up in time."

Ben nods and then goes back to typing on his computer, but I feel his eyes on me as I walk out of his office.

Chapter 3

Waking up with the sun the next morning, I stretch out in bed, ready for the long day ahead of me.

After showering, I stand in front of my suitcases, trying to decide what to put on. I go with tight black skinny jeans, black suede booties, and an oversized cream sweater that I tuck in the front of my jeans. Adding my belt that has a gold interlocking G logo, I layer a few gold chain necklaces around my neck and slip on rings and earrings to finish off my look.

Blow-drying my hair, I straighten it and then apply my makeup, ready to take on the day.

Yesterday, I placed fifty boxes of white lightbulb style string lights on hold at the nearest large box store, and made sure to call in two of the warehouse guys from back in

Toronto to come and help me hang them. Since it's Wednesday, they aren't needed for any transport until an event tomorrow.

Fifty boxes of lights turn out to be a much larger haul than I pictured in my head, and I struggle to get it all in my car and then inside the winery. I don't know where to store them while we're working, so I go in search of Ben to ask if I can use one of the rooms off in the right wing where they hold larger events.

It's still early, only about eight in the morning, so I'm hoping he's here. I knock on his office door, but there's no answer.

"Good morning," Ben says from right behind me, his husky voice making me jump.

"Oh," I gasp, startled. "I didn't hear you come up behind me." My heart is beating wildly in my chest, and doesn't settle when I look at him. He's in a pair of dark rinse jeans and a grey sweater that makes him look like a hot department store model and gives his blue eyes a steely effect.

"Sorry," he apologizes, the corners of his mouth turning down. "Did you need me for something?"

"I wanted to ask if I could use one of the event spaces to house the boxes of lights as I work today. I have them in the tasting room, but I don't want them there for when people arrive for the day."

"Sure, go ahead. We don't have any events today."

"Alright, thanks."

I go to walk past him, but Ben steps up onto the

platform from the last step, blocking my way with his large frame. "Will you need help? I don't want you hanging them all by yourself."

"I wasn't going to. I've already called in a couple guys from the company who are driving down from Toronto. They should be here soon. They have experience rigging things up for events."

"Good." He nods, stepping to the side for me. I still have to brush past him to get to the stairs, and an electric current zaps up my arm and down my spine from that simple touch. We're fully clothed with no skin touching, and yet I feel it as if we were naked. And I want more.

My eyes find his over my shoulder and I feel their depth, swimming with secrets he doesn't let surface. But I want to pull them out of him. I want to understand him. Despite his success, he carries himself like a damaged man with wounds he's still licking.

Gripping the railing, I put more weight on it as I descend the stairs, needing it to keep my balance, all the while feeling Ben's eyes on me. Even when I'm out of his sightline, I still feel them on me like a blanket of warmth, heating me from the inside out.

But it could all just be in my head.

I'm a confident woman 90% of the time, loving my curves and loving the fact that I don't look like I've been going hungry. I'm an independent, educated woman who knows what she wants in life. I know how to dress to my figure and carry myself with my head held high. I don't let anyone get me down or tear me down. But with a man like

Ben Breaker… He's a gorgeous, wealthy, famous ex-hockey player who could have any woman he wants. Although when he looks at me, I can't tell if he's looking at me like an annoyance or looking at me with the heat of a man who wants me.

My phone ringing in my back pocket pulls me from my thoughts, and I see it's one of the warehouse guys. "Hey, Anton. Are you here?"

"Yeah, we're outside. We wanted to know where to go and where to bring the ladder."

"There's a path to the left of the building that will take you to between the distillery and the main building. I'll meet you out there."

"Okay." Disconnecting the call, I grab as many bags of light boxes as I can and head outside.

"Hey, Leah." Anton greets with a smile, carrying a twenty-four-foot ladder with George.

"Hi, guys." I smile back. "I hope you're ready for a long day of stringing up lights!" I say excitedly, and they both huff out polite laughs.

"Just tell us what you need and we'll take care of it."

After going over everything I need from them, I start to unbox and unwind the strings of lights while they set up the hooks needed to hold them all along the roof and poles of the ice rink. The rink is already lit by a few flood lights on the trim of the distillery and winery's buildings, but they're so harsh. These lights will be much softer and more welcoming.

We're halfway done when my hands start to go numb out in the freezing cold air. "Who's ready for a break?" I ask, looking up at George and Anton on the latter and roof. "My hands are about to fall off and I'm starving."

"Us, too. We'll be down in a minute."

Nodding, I stuff my hands in my pockets, waiting for them before heading inside and through to the kitchen. "Hi, Chef." I smile, walking past him to the coffee station.

"Hi, Leah." He returns my grin with a lopsided one of his own. "I saw you guys working out there. Can I make you something?"

"Oh, that'd be great. As long as it isn't any trouble."

"Not at all," he assures me. "Grab a coffee or tea to warm up and look over the menu. I'll make you three whatever you'd like."

My smile is instant. "Thank you so much."

"And I'll have the lobster bisque ready for you later," he adds.

"Perfect."

We eat our lunch out in the restaurant area where a few other tables are occupied by patrons, and then get back to work outside once we've thawed out.

We continue on for the rest of the afternoon, and it's not until after the sun has set and the stars come out that we're finally finished.

"Oh my God, I love it," I breathe, smiling up at the lights against the night sky. "Thank you so much. It looks amazing and you guys are amazing for doing this in one day."

"You're welcome, Leah. You know we'd do anything for you," George says, nudging my arm.

"Thank you." I give them each a smile and a hug,

walking them back around to the company truck. "Drive safe!" I call out before they drive off.

Pulling my hat down further on my head, I shove my fists in my pockets and walk back around to the ice rink, smiling up at the lights again.

"It looks good," Ben's deep voice rumbles right behind me.

"I know." I'm still smiling when I look over at him, and his eyes roam over my face. "Thank you for letting me do this."

He gives a small nod. "Casey left you a container of bisque so you can have your own tasting."

"Oh, good. I've been looking forward to it."

"Do you mind if I join you?"

Surprised, my eyes widen, and I take a beat to form words. "Yeah. Yes. Sure. Of course," I babble. "I need you to show me which wine it's being paired with anyhow."

Following him inside the restaurant door, he gestures to the tables. "Have a seat."

Sitting down, I take off my hat and scarf, but I'm not exactly ready to take off my jacket yet.

"Here you go," Ben says a few minutes later, placing a cup of soup in front of me. "I'll get the wine."

"Thank you." The smell of sweet lobster bisque floats up into my nostrils and I close my eyes, trying to decipher the various ingredients.

"Something wrong?"

My eyes pop open to find Ben looking at me, his brows drawn together in concern. "No. I was just taking in the aroma." Clearing my throat, I reach for the small glass of wine he placed in front of me. "Tell me about your Vidal. I have to be honest with you, I've never had icewine, and I don't know much about it."

"Take a sip, then I can explain the process."

Swirling my glass, I breathe it in with my mouth slightly open, then take a small sip, sweet flavors immediately bursting on my tongue. "Oh, that's not what I was expecting," I tell him, surprised.

"Is that a good thing?"

I laugh lightly. "Yes, it is. It's sweet, but not overabundantly so. I'm not a fan of those sickly-sweet girly drinks. With this, my mind actually goes straight to sitting outside by a fire, roasting marshmallows for s'mores." I take another sip. "The cold sweetness would taste good with it, I think."

The corners of Ben's lips twitch and I hold my breath for a second, thinking he might smile. He doesn't, though. "Was this pairing your idea?" I ask, gliding my spoon through the bisque.

"No. It was my mom's favorite, and it was her idea when the festival began almost three decades ago."

"You never thought of changing it up?" My question is meant to be innocent, but I see my mistake when Ben's eyes flare.

"No. Why fix what's not broken? People love the bisque. They expect the bisque."

"I didn't mean any offense," I defend. "It was just a question. I realize you don't like change."

"No, I don't."

"And why's that?" I ask, seeing if I can get him to open up even the slightest.

His eyes bore into mine. "I have my reasons."

"Alright." I brush off his brisk attitude. What he doesn't realize about me is that I'm patient when it comes to people. That's why I usually get handed the brides and clients no one else wants to work with. I can wear even the toughest cookie down by simply being kind, listening, and waiting.

"I was going through Janet's schedule and I saw a shipment of lobsters is supposed to come in tomorrow morning. Will there be time to make enough bisque for the weekend?"

"Half the shipment came yesterday, and Casey has made enough for Friday and part of Saturday."

"Tell me about the process of making icewine. I don't want to be ignorant when I talk to people," I confess, lifting my glass to my lips.

Leaning back in his chair, Ben holds his glass up to the light, studying the liquid before taking a sip. "We leave the grapes on the vine past our regular harvest. Sometimes months. It isn't until the first freeze that we harvest them, and it's precise. We have a team on call and it's usually in the middle of the night or early morning when we have to act quick to pick the vines before they're too far gone and we can't extract any juice from them."

"Is there a certain temperature you wait until so that you know it's almost time?"

"Yes. By law, it has to be at least -8°C, and the window of time to pick can be as short as a few hours. If we miss the window, then the grapes will be too hard for the equipment. And if the freeze comes too late in the year, then the grapes could rot on the vine before we have a chance to harvest."

Looking down at my glass, I study the pretty, light gold liquid.

"Leaving them on the vines longer allows the water in the grapes to freeze. The sugars in them don't, though, which leads to a higher concentrated juice to be pressed from them. Because of that, there's less of it, which means more grapes are needed per bottle and a lower yield of finished product."

"Which means you can charge more." I smile, taking another sip.

"Yes, and we also have to in order to make a profit."

"So, because the sugars don't freeze, it makes it sweeter?"

"Yes, exactly." The look in his eyes while he's talking about the work he does has me wanting him to never stop. He looks relaxed. He looks…softer? Less of a grumpy stuck-in-his-ways man.

"Do you make any other icewine varietals?"

Nodding, Ben finishes off his soup. "We also make a Riesling. Would you like to try it?"

"I would. But maybe tomorrow? I'm exhausted from today." I would love to sit here with him longer, but my exhaustion from being outside all day is starting to kick in and I really just want to crawl into bed and pass out.

"Of course," he says quickly, and with how open he was before, I see him close himself off again.

My God, this man is a tough nut to crack.

Chapter 4

"Hi, Charlie."

"Good morning, Leah. How are you?"

"Good, thank you. Today is fire pit day," I say excitedly, rubbing my hands together.

"Sounds fun," he says on a laugh, pulling out bottles of whiskey from a crate.

"It's going to be great," I assure him. Heading into the kitchen to make myself a cup of coffee before I tackle the fire pits outside, the sound of yelling stops me in my tracks.

Oh no.

"What do you mean they can't get another shipment here? We need them! What are we supposed to serve people?" Ben's voice booms loudly through the kitchen, and as I step around the corner, I see him and Chef Casey in a heated discussion.

"The truck broke down a hundred miles away and the cargo is ruined. I've called all available sellers and they can't bring me the amount I need until next week."

Ben's face turns red as he mutters a string of curses under his breath, slicing his fingers through his hair.

"What's going on?" I ask gently.

Both sets of eyes dart to mine, and while every instinct in me wants to shrink back, I stand tall.

"The lobster shipment isn't coming and we don't have a backup plan," Chef Casey says gently, as if repeating it will set Ben off again.

"I may sound ignorant suggesting this, but can't we just drive around and buy out all the lobsters in every store that carries them?"

"You're right, that is ignorant," Ben snipes, and I clamp my mouth shut.

"Hey," Chef Casey says, "don't take it out on her. She's just trying to help."

Ben looks over at me again and his whole demeanor changes, realizing what he said. "I shouldn't have said that."

"It's fine."

"No, it's not." He shakes his head. "We can't do that because there aren't enough places that stock lobsters in January, and even if we could manage to round up enough, we wouldn't have enough time to make the bisque."

"Then we need another plan."

"And what? You have one?" Ben asks incredulously, his

condescending tone making me want to slap some manners into him.

"Yes, I do," I tell him, lifting my chin defiantly. "Last night when we were tasting the wine, I had an idea, but I didn't dare mention it because I know how much you *love* change."

Chef Casey smirks. "She has you pegged. What was your idea?"

"When I think of an icewine festival, I think of a winter wonderland. And when I think of a winter wonderland, I think of hot chocolate, ice skating, lights, and snow. You have an ice rink, we added the lights yesterday, there's already snow on the ground, and when I was in New York City one December, I went to this bakery that was famous for their hot chocolate and massive marshmallows. It was like eating a sugar cloud of deliciousness."

Ben blinks, his face blank like he can't believe I just said what I did. "What are you suggesting? That we have our guests eat marshmallows with our wine?"

"Yes. I told you last night it made me think of s'mores. But I think just the marshmallows would be perfect."

"It's not a bad idea," Chef Casey interjects. "I've made them before, and adding icewine to the recipe is simple and will only aide in the sweetness."

"You can't be serious," Ben deadpans.

"Why are you so dismissive of it? Just because it's my first time here doesn't mean I can't have a good idea. Picture your guests outside around the fire pits, laughing and enjoying the cold and snow, watching people skate while roasting giant marshmallows. I'd pay for that."

Ben is quiet for a long moment, the wheels in his head spinning as he rubs his jaw. "Fine," he concedes, but I can tell how much it pains him. "Make a batch so I can try it."

I wish I could stick my tongue out and tell him to shove it, but I'm not a child and this isn't an elementary school playground. Instead, I take the small victory with grace. "I'm going to get started on putting together the fire pits."

"Do you have help again today?"

"No, I'll be fine."

"I'll help," he insists, and I give him a cautious look.

"Alright. If you're not busy." I have no problem doing them myself, but it'll go much faster with Ben, and save my fingers from frostbite.

"Well, our entire weekend and reputation is riding on these fire pits now, so I better help."

"That's the spirit," I tease, fighting the urge to roll my eyes. I catch Chef Casey's smile as I turn to leave, gulping my coffee as I go to ensure I'm caffeinated enough to deal with working with Ben for the entire day.

Walking outside, I find the boxes of fire pits stacked neatly under the awning of the patio. I made sure to tell the delivery guys to bring them around back so I wouldn't have to figure out how to drag them out here myself.

"I ordered these nice gas ones for you so you don't have to worry about stocking wood or having someone go around to make sure the flames don't die down. They also have a tiled ledge around them so people will have a place to rest their glasses if needed."

He studies the picture on one of the boxes. "They look good."

Smiling to myself, I reach to pull the first box down. He's such a grump, begrudgingly throwing me an ounce of praise.

"Hey, hey, I got it," he insists, pushing his way in front of me to get the box down himself.

"I'm fully capable of carrying heavy boxes."

"I never said you weren't. I'm just being nice."

"That'd be refreshing."

Ben puts the box down and his eyes find mine. "I'm just used to Janet handling everything."

"I get that, but I'm here to help, and I see so much potential in your winery when it comes to this festival. And while I realize that a few days before the event isn't the time to voice those ideas, maybe when this is all over, you'll let me make a few suggestions for next year."

Ben runs a hand through his hair. "Sure. We'll see."

Yeah, I know what that means.

Sighing, I take a seat on one of the benches by the rink and get to work unboxing and putting together the first one.

Ben and I work in silence for a while, and more often than not, I feel his eyes on me, watching me. I don't know if it's because he thinks I can't put together a damned fire pit and he's checking to make sure I'm doing it right, or for some other reason, but my hands are shaking under his scrutiny.

"Stop doing that," I finally say to him.

"Doing what?"

"I can feel you watching me."

"Am I making you nervous?" Did his voice just drop even lower?

"I know what I'm doing. I don't need to you doubting every single thing I do."

"I don't doubt you."

"You do." I lift my eyes to his. "You can't deny that. I'm not stupid, Ben. I just don't understand why you dismiss me at every turn and speak to me as if I'm a child."

Staring at each other, my breaths come short and quick. I don't know why I'm letting him get to me like this. Probably because despite the way he's treated me, I want to know what lies beneath that hard mask he wears. I've also never wanted to know what a man tastes like as much as I do with Ben. Those full lips he keeps in a tight line, and those taut muscles he's hiding under his sweaters…

My mouth waters.

Ben's midnight blue eyes swirl and my head does the same. "I'm going to get a coffee," I announce, standing abruptly.

"Leah, wait."

I stop in my tracks, but keep my back to him. "We have to work together for the next few weeks and I don't want things to be awkward or filled with tension. I know you're used to Janet and you don't like that I'm here, but I'm here to do my job, and I'm going to do it well. Now, if you'll excuse me, I need a coffee break."

He doesn't try and stop me this time and I'm thankful. Even just being in the same vicinity as him puts me on edge.

❄ ❄ ❄ ❄

My fingers are numb. Two days in a row now, I've spent the entire day outside in the freezing cold, and I'm starting to feel it bone deep, as if I'll never get warm.

Ben and I just finished putting together ten fire pits and placing them around the patio area of the ice rink. They look really good and have made the entire outdoor area into a welcoming place for people to gather and enjoy the winter weather.

I let Ben take the lead in hooking up the propane tanks, and after turning them all on to test them, I take a seat beside the last one near The Whiskey Room's door, rubbing my hands together as close to the flames as possible.

"I thought you could use this." A glass of wine appears in my peripheral vision, and I look up to see Ben holding two glasses of red wine.

"Thank you." I take the glass from him and our fingers brush lightly, sending a jolt of electricity through me, instantly warming me more than the fire.

He takes the seat across from me and I catch glimpses of his handsome face between the flames that lick up to the night sky. Why does he have to be thoughtful and nice after being an ass?

"Did Chef Casey make the marshmallows yet?"

"Yes. I tried one."

"You did? Why didn't you bring me one?" I meant it to sound like a joke, but it came out sounding more like an accusation. "Don't you think we should roast them out here with a glass of icewine to get the full experience and make sure it's as delicious as I thought it'd be?"

Ben's eyes dance in the flames. "I should've thought of that. After this glass, I'll go get us what we need."

Hiding my smile behind my own glass, I take a long sip and let the wine warm my insides the way being near the big grumbling man in front of me does.

I'm beginning to like sniping with him.

Placing my empty glass down on the ledge of the fire pit, I lean back and cross my legs, smiling. "I'm ready for my tasting now."

"I can see that." The smirk on his face makes my stomach knot and then take flight with a thousand little butterflies. "I'll be right back."

When he comes back with a tray in hand, I don't bother hiding my smile. "I'm not going to lie, I'm really excited to try one," I tell him, eyeing the giant marshmallows on the plate. "I've had dreams of the ones from the city."

Ben hands me a long metal roasting stick and I choose the biggest marshmallow on the plate to start with, spearing it on the end. Holding it over the open flame, I watch the outside begin to bubble and char before pulling it out and blowing on it. I have to quickly take a bite before it falls apart, and when the sugary goodness melts on my tongue, I groan.

"Ohmygod," I say in a rush, laughing, covering my mouth with my hand. "This is amazing."

Ben's lips twitch, fighting the urge to smile. "Glad you approve." He places his own in the fire, and when he takes a bite, it sticks to his lip, and I can't take my eyes off the white sweetness stuck to him that everything in me is screaming to go over and lick off.

His tongue peeks out to run over his bottom lip and he captures what I want to claim as my own, scraping his teeth over it to ensure he gets it all.

Oh, sweet baby Jesus.

Is it hot out here?

My throat just went dry and my body flares alive like the fire in front of me. I want to know what it would be like to have his tongue lick across my lips like that before he bites them.

I swallow the moan threatening to bubble up and out of me and avert my eyes to the stones around the flames.

I gulp down half my wine to try and cool myself off before I do or say something that will totally ruin the professionalism I know I need to maintain around him. Although, professionalism kind of flew out the window the moment I gave him a piece of my mind that first day.

"I think everyone's going to love this," I tell him, my eyes finding his again through the flames.

"Me too."

"I'll send out an email to the head of the festival so they can change our pairing on the website." Ben nods. "I know you're skeptical of everything, but I promise I'm going to make sure Breaker Estates is the most memorable stop on everyone's tour."

"I'm sure you will." His words are devoid of sarcasm, but I know he's still doubtful of me. I'm going to prove him wrong.

"Thank you for helping me today. I know you probably had a lot to do."

"Nothing I can't do tonight."

"Oh, tonight? I'm sorry to keep you. I should go."

"You don't have to," he assures me.

"I do. I want to be rested for opening day."

"Are you going to the gala tomorrow night?"

"No? Am I supposed to?"

"I guess Janet didn't tell you you're invited. Each participating winery is given a packet of passes for everyone involved in the event."

"Are you going?"

"No. Casey, Charlie, and Kate are going, though. I never go."

"Why?"

"Not my scene."

"Do you ever show your face?" I ask without thought.

"What do you mean?"

"I mean," I drag out the word, "you were a famous professional hockey player who doesn't want to capitalize on that for your business."

"I think our products and this place should speak for themselves. It isn't about me."

"But if you made it about you even just a little, then—"

"No," he says quickly, cutting me off. "I'm done with that life. I don't want to be out in front of the camera and have people thinking they know me or have a right to know me because I played hockey."

"Do you have anyone that you let see you? Know you?" The words are out of my mouth before I can stop them.

Ben's eyes hold mine captive, rubbing his jaw before answering. "No."

"You have to sometime, Ben. Your gruff, hard exterior that tells the world to eff-off and stay away will leave you alone forever." I can't believe I just said that.

"I like being alone."

"So do I. But I don't always want to be alone." I take another sip of wine, which has clearly loosened my tongue. "There's a difference between being alone and being lonely."

"Are you lonely?" he asks, those three little words asking so damn much. But if I want him to show me what's beneath his exterior, I have to show him what's beneath mine.

"Yes," I tell him honestly. "Sometimes. I've been alone most of my life, focused on my career and achieving every goal I've set for myself. I don't let myself dwell on it too much, though. I know I won't be alone forever. My life motto has always been, 'one day'. One day everything I want and have worked for will be mine. One day I'll fall in love. One day I'll travel."

"I can tell you're the kind of person who will get everything she wants in life."

"I'm going to choose to take that as a compliment and not some weird backhanded insult."

"It was a compliment."

The icewine is cool and sweet as it slides down my throat and spreads through me, tamping down the fire I feel burning in my chest.

Clearing my throat, I look away. "I should go. I want to have more than just a marshmallow for dinner. I will take another one for later, though." I place my glass down and stand, swiping a marshmallow from the plate.

"See you tomorrow, Leah."

"See you tomorrow, Ben." Making a quick exit, I go inside and grab my bag before heading out to my car.

Chapter 5

"Hi, everyone," I greet the waitstaff as I walk into the winery the next morning. "Are we ready for today?" I get a ring of yeses in reply as I place my purse behind the check-in table at the top of the ramp.

Since The Whiskey Room is closed during the festival, the servers will be working with me as cocktail waiters and waitresses to ensure the tasting room remains pristine and everyone is happy and has a full glass of whatever they're drinking.

I'll be the one checking everyone in as they arrive, marking off the stop on their passes and giving them a pamphlet on Breaker Estates before directing them to the table beside me to get their marshmallow and glass of icewine.

"Oh good, the flowers were delivered." Walking over to one of the tables, I pick up the mason jar and inspect the bouquet of ruscus greenery and baby's breath. Simple, yet clean and classy, tying everything together nicely.

To say I'm nervous would be an understatement. Despite how Ben was last night, I know I still have something to prove.

When I've inspected every inch of the tasting room, I direct a couple of staff to go outside and wipe down the tables and chairs and turn on the fire pits.

"Good morning, Leah." Ben's deep voice slides through me like a warm caress, and I turn to find him leaning against the bar.

Giving him a small smile, I nervously tuck a strand of hair behind my ear. "Good morning."

"I brought you a coffee. I thought you might need it."

"Oh, yes, thank you. That was so thoughtful," I say, surprised, taking the to-go cup from him. It has the logo from the café where we first met on it.

Clearing his throat, Ben runs a hand through his hair. "Have you given any more thought to the gala tonight?"

"You mean if I'm going to go?" Why is he so interested in if I'm going?

He nods. "Yeah."

"Oh, not really. I wouldn't know anyone there, and I didn't bring anything to wear to a fancy event."

"You'd look beautiful in anything," he says, the deep rumble of his words flowing through me and settling low in my belly. "The winery has a table. So, if you decide to go"—he hands me a ticket from his back pocket—"then you'll need this."

"How about this... I'll go if you go." I smile. "You seem like you could use a little fun in your life. You can't spend all of your time in your office."

The corners of his lips lift just the slightest. "Fine. You have a deal."

My smile turns into a full-blown grin. That wasn't as hard of a sell as I thought it would be. "Good."

❋ ❋ ❋ ❋

Stepping out of the shower, I wipe the steam from the mirror and study my blurry reflection.

Today was a success. Everything went smoothly and the marshmallows were a huge hit. I loved seeing how everyone gathered together outside, laughing and having fun like they were kids again, roasting marshmallows at camp. Except way classier, and with wine.

Digging through my suitcases, I pull out a black dress I remember throwing in there as a 'just in case' dress. Just in case of what? I wasn't sure. But now I guess it was for tonight.

It's not as fancy as I would've chosen for a gala, but it is one of my favorites, and I'll just dress it up with a few extra jewelry pieces to make it feel fancier.

I go through the motions of drying my hair and curling it into loose waves, then apply my makeup, playing up my eyes so the gold flecks inside the brown have a chance to shine. Shrugging off my silk robe, I slip my dress over my head and pull it down into place. It hits just above my knees, and the off-the-shoulder fit and flare style makes my waist appear smaller and allows my hips and behind the room they need. Choosing a pair of black suede heeled booties that will ensure my toes don't freeze off when walking outside, I zip them up and stand in front of the mirror.

I love fashion and dressing up, and I do have to admit that I look good. I love the way this dress looks on me and how it makes me feel. Confident and sexy. I'm not going to lie, I hope I get a reaction out of Ben.

I place the ticket he gave me this morning in my small clutch and then don my jacket and scarf before heading out into the cold.

When I arrive at the Niagara Falls Resort and Casino, I follow the signs around the casino until I find the ballroom where the gala is being held.

Oh, wow.

Everything is white, silver, and covered in glitter or fake snow, with a dozen or so snow flocked trees lining the outer walls of the room, all decorated in white and silver ornaments, ribbon, and décor.

Icy crystals hang from the chandeliers by silver bows, while a real ice sculpture takes the stage as the showpiece between the buffet tables.

The centerpieces are a mix of tall and short arrangements of white roses, holly berry branches, and flocked balsam branches. The taller ones have white ostrich plume feathers that add depth, and crystals dripping from the rim of the vase's openings.

Everything is so beautiful.

Scanning the room, I spot a table that has Charlie with his arm around a beautiful woman, Kate sitting beside a man who looks to be her husband, and Chef Casey by himself, and I walk towards them.

"Leah, you decided to come!" Charlie says jovially, a huge grin on his face. I eye the drink in his hand and begin to believe that isn't his first. "I'd like you to meet my fiancé, Laura."

"Hi, and yes, I did. Ben and I made a deal."

"What kind of a deal?"

"I said I would come if he did." That gets a round of laughs from everyone. "What?"

"Ben never comes to the gala. He used to with his parents a few times, but not in some time," Kate tells me, knowing him the longest.

"Well, be prepared to be surprised. I told him he needed to get out of his office."

"Hmm," she hums. "It seems Leah has a way of getting Ben to do things."

"No, I don't," I deny, but feel my cheeks heat under their scrutiny.

"You got him to change our featured food," Chef Casey says.

"That was out of necessity," I defend, and he laughs.

"No. Ben would've made me and the entire kitchen staff drive around and buy every lobster in a hundred-mile radius if you hadn't suggested otherwise."

"He agreed that it was stupid to suggest that."

"Exactly. He was too proud to admit that that was going to be the next words out of his mouth."

"Typical Ben." Kate smiles, shaking her head. "I'm glad to know that the big bear can still change his ways. Speaking of..." she trails off, looking over my shoulder.

Turning around, I have to make sure my jaw doesn't fall off when I see Ben walking towards me. His tall, broad frame, is clad in a dark suit that makes him look like every woman's fantasy come to life. Well, at least *this* woman's every fantasy.

His messy hair is tamed and combed back, giving me a full view of his handsome face. He even trimmed his beard so it's down to just a shadow, and oh my Lord, I want to feel it against my skin. His rugged good looks are even amplified by his slightly crooked nose with a little bump on the bridge, probably from being broken one too many times in hockey.

Every step he takes exudes confidence and a sureness of who he is, and when my eyes finish their perusal of his suit-clad body, my eyes lock with his deep midnight blue ones. The corner of his mouth lifts in a sexy little smirk that lets me know he knows I was checking him out. Which would normally make me blush and look away at being caught, but his eyes won't let me. They're holding mine captive.

When he's only a few steps from me, his eyes run down my body and back up, a hunger in them that makes my core clench with need and my stomach knot with nerves.

"You came," I say, my voice barely above a whisper.

"A deal's a deal."

"Good to see you out in the world, Ben!" Charlie says loudly, stepping forward to shake his hand and slap his back.

"Why does everyone think I'm a shut-in?"

"Because you are. If we knew all you needed was a pretty woman to drag you out, I would've found you one years ago," Chef Casey jokes, but Ben's eyes shoot daggers at him.

"How about we get a drink?" I offer, and Ben gives me a curt nod.

We walk beside each other to the bar, and when we get closer to the small crowd in line, he places his hand on my lower back, startling me. Biting my lower lip, my eyes dart up to his, but he's looking straight ahead.

"What would you like?" he asks when we reach the front.

"A glass of red wine, please."

"88 whiskey neat and a glass of Breaker's Cabernet," he tells the bartender.

"You're ordering your own stuff?" I ask, smiling up at him.

"Why not? I make it. I like it."

"It's just funny to hear you order it, is all. I haven't gotten to try your whiskey yet."

"Make that two 88 whiskeys and the cab," he tells the bartender.

Ben takes the whiskey glasses and I grab the wine glass held out for me, and we make our way to an empty high-top table near the charcuterie display.

"Do you ever drink whiskey?" he asks, sliding one of the

glasses closer to me.

"I've had it before, if that's what you're asking. But only a couple of times."

"Did you like it?"

"Not really. But then again, it wasn't the good stuff. I'm hoping yours will change my mind."

His eyes heat at my words and I look down at the amber liquid, away from his scrutiny.

Bringing the glass to my lips, I inhale the sweet scent, scrunching my nose at the slight burn to my nostrils, which makes Ben smile.

Oh. My. God.

I think my heart just stopped.

"Well? Are you going to try it?"

"What?" I breathe, too distracted by how his face transforms when he smiles.

"Why are you staring at me like that?"

"What?" I say again, like a babbling idiot. Peeling my eyes away from his mouth, I find his eyes dancing with humor like I haven't seen yet. "Oh, sorry." My cheeks warm, but I decide to own the fact that I was staring. "You distracted me. I haven't seen you smile yet and it threw me for a loop." Smirking, I take a small sip of whiskey and cough as it slides down my throat. "I wasn't expecting that," I say, covering my mouth on another cough. "It's strong."

"It's supposed to be," he says, taking a sip from his own glass.

I take another one, this time prepared for the burn, and instead of coughing, I actually taste the sweet and smokiness of the whiskey. "Huh, not bad."

"Remind me to give you a tasting at the distillery one day. Each one we make has a different aging process and taste to them."

"I'm going to hold you to that."

The lights dim and brighten, signaling for us to take our seats. Ben places his hand on my lower back again and I feel his touch through the fabric of my dress, making me wish I knew what it felt like to have him touch me with nothing between us.

Taking our seats, I ignore the looks the others are giving us, and instead unfold my napkin and place it on my lap.

A woman comes out onto the dance floor and introduces herself as the head of the Niagara Region Wine Committee. "Welcome everyone to this year's Icewine Gala! We have representatives from all 29 of our participating wineries, as well as those who love wine and parties as much as we do! Raise your glasses to a night of good food, wine, and dancing!" she exclaims, raising her glass in the air. "Please enjoy yourselves!"

Ben lifts his to mine, clinking our glasses together, his eyes holding a mischievous glint.

After dinner, Ben goes to the bar to get the both of us another round of drinks, and I see a few people approach him on his way back. I almost forgot he's famous. Growing up here, he became a local hero and inspiration when he was drafted to the NHL, and it's well-known that he took over Breaker Estates. But Ben's reaction to the attention is nothing short of standoffish, and by the looks on the couple's faces, I can tell they're disappointed in his response to them.

Standing, I make my way over to him. "Fans of yours?"

"Yeah," he grunts out.

Sighing, I place my hand on my hip. "I figured as much. Ben, you were rude to them. I saw their faces."

"You don't know anything."

"I know that they were brave enough to approach you and you gave them the cold shoulder like you did me when you thought I was a fan. They looked disappointed."

"I don't like attention. It's why I don't go to these things."

"I get that it can be bothersome to be interrupted or recognized, but you can't keep hiding, and you can't be mean to people just trying to say hi. I know you're capable of being nice," I tell him gently, "so I think you should try it more often."

"You don't know me, Leah," he says harshly.

"Right," I say, nodding once and looking away. He doesn't let anyone know him.

Taking the glass of wine he got for me from his hand, I spin around and head back to the table, muttering where I'd like to throw this drink if not for the fact that I want to actually drink it.

For a second earlier, I thought that maybe Ben was different, but he proved again that he's more of a cranky ass than I gave him credit for.

Sitting back down, I take a giant gulp of wine and hope it settles the annoyance building in me. I don't even know why it bothers me so much that Ben is the way he is. It just does.

When the music changes to a slower song, I feel Ben beside me again, sliding his hand down the side of my arm, gaining my attention.

Gone is the anger and annoyance from his eyes, but that doesn't mean it's gone from mine. "Dance with me," he states.

"That wasn't a question."

"Will you dance with me?" he asks instead, and I blow out a breath.

"Aren't you worried people will stare at, or bother, you?"

"If I'm dancing with you, trust me, they won't be staring at me." His words melt my anger, and I find myself nodding as he takes my hand, walking us out onto the dance floor. It's filled with a decent amount of people, but I don't even see them as Ben lifts my arms around his neck and wraps his around my waist.

With only a fraction of space between us, I can smell his cologne, and my head spins at the intoxicating scent.

Everything about him is intoxicating.

My eyes stare at his chin, not daring to look any higher, choosing to study the light shadow of his beard instead, wishing I could skim my lips over it to feel the soft prickle.

"I'm sorry," he begins, and my eyes move to his lips, up the bridge of his nose, and then dart between his eyes. "I shouldn't have been short with you. And I know I've done it a few times already—"

"Yes, you have," I interrupt, but there's no malice in my tone. I can see the sincerity of regret in his eyes.

"I'm just not used to needing or wanting to justify myself to anyone."

"What do you mean? Why would you have to feel like that with me?" Sliding my fingers back and forth across the fabric of his suit at the nape of his neck, I lock them together before I'm dumb enough to give in to the urge to reach up and slide them through his hair.

Instead of answering me, Ben reaches up and grabs one of my hands. Gripping my hip with the other, he spins me out and away from him, and I'm so caught off guard, that when he pulls me back against him, the breath is knocked out of me.

There's no space between us now.

His hard chest feels like a wall of muscle against mine, and my nipples harden instantly.

I don't know the last time I was this close to a man.

I broke up with my ex over a year ago, and he certainly wasn't a man like Ben Breaker, and my body never lit up this way from just dancing with him, either. That alone should've been the first red flag with him, and not have waited to break up with him until he 'suggested' I go to the gym more so my legs could look even better in my dresses...

No thank you.

My legs are shapely and sexy, and if I wanted to spend endless hours in a gym working on them, then I would. But I don't.

It's not true love when a man says he really likes you and finds your confidence sexy, then comes back around to say you would be so much more beautiful if you worked out and lost a little weight…

I'm paraphrasing, but he did say that to me one night when I said in passing that I hadn't been to the gym in a while.

But Jon was like that. Everything always had a 'but' after it when he complimented me, and I got sick of it. The only 'but' there should be when complimenting me is the slap to mine after he says how sexy I look.

But that was over a year ago, and I honestly never think of him anymore. Until now. Because with Ben holding me close like this, I feel everything, but I don't dare say anything for fear this moment will turn out to all be in my head.

I want to believe that the heartbeat I feel pounding isn't just my own with our chests pressed together, but that's just wishful thinking. It also might be the whiskey and wine in my bloodstream making me think that Ben is feeling this too.

The song ends, and the next one has a fast tempo, so I regretfully take a step back. We stand there for a moment and I look up at him, unable to read his eyes.

"I'm, uhm, thirsty," I say lamely. "I'm going to go back to the table."

I know I'm acting like a coward, running back to the table and the safety of the others, but I don't know if I'm ready to feel everything I was feeling in Ben's arms. He's not someone I should ever get involved with. For starters, he's a client. And secondly…well, my mind is coming up blank because I can still feel his arms around me.

Finishing off my glass of wine, I look back on the dance floor and see Ben talking to a couple of people, this time not ignoring them, but rather engaging in a conversation where his face doesn't look like he wishes he were anywhere else.

Huh, maybe he's not as hopeless as he seems, but I still can't give in to whatever I feel when I'm around him. I have to stay professional. And dancing with our bodies pressed together is most definitely *not* professional.

"Alright, guys, I'm going to get going," I tell the table, hoping I can slip out without Ben noticing.

"No, Leah. Stay!" Charlie insists, and his fiancé rolls her eyes, laughing at his drunkenness.

"I should go. I've had a long week and am exhausted."

"Alright, we'll see you tomorrow," Chef Casey says, leaning in to kiss me on the cheek, catching me off guard.

I weave through the room and am out in the lobby wrapping my scarf around my neck by the coat check when I feel him behind me.

"You were going to leave without saying goodbye?" Ben asks, handing his ticket to the women behind the desk.

"I'm just tired."

"Then I should drive you home."

"Oh, no, you don't have to do that. I drove here, and I'm fine to drive back."

"Are you sure?"

No, I'm not.

"Yes, I'm fine. Thank you, though. I'll see you tomorrow." Hurrying outside, I use the blast of cold air to slap some sense into me as I walk around to the outer entrance of the garage.

Sitting in my car, I close my eyes and take a deep breath,

leaning my head back against the headrest.

I can't go there with him. I don't even know what made him change earlier. He went from cold and standoffish to being sweet and holding me close.

There seems to be this low electric current between us that calls to the other, and when he touched me tonight, that current turned into a full-blown storm of need swirling through me, settling in my core.

I can't let my body's needs cloud my judgement, though. This is my chance to add to my portfolio and prove to my aunt that she really can trust me to handle anything. And getting involved with a client isn't a part of the plan. No matter that the client is a 6'4" broody man with a face that could make angels weep.

When I've calmed my rapid heartbeat back down to a steady thumping, I start my car and make my way back to the inn. I just hope sleep comes quick and the morning brings with it the restraint I desperately need to be around Ben.

Chapter 6

I was able to successfully avoid Ben all day yesterday and today. The winery was busy beyond belief, and I barely had a second to myself to even go to the bathroom or eat lunch, much less have a moment to talk to Ben.

I've seen him from across the room when he's come down to look around, but he remained hidden behind the bar. I guess Friday night was enough face-time for him with the public and now he's back to keeping his distance.

By the end of Sunday, I'm dead on my feet as I walk around the ice rink to tell the few people left out here that we're closing. Although I'm finally getting a moment to step outside, and it's refreshing to breathe in the cold air.

Snow has been steadily falling all day, but it hasn't

deterred anyone from coming out here to roast their marshmallows. Most haven't stayed and sat, deciding to have another glass of wine inside. But some have, while others opted to have a skate under the falling flakes.

I watch the couple holding hands and skating together for a moment before I have to tell them we're closing. She has a massive smile on her face, her head uplifted to the star-studded sky while her man looks at her with nothing but love shining in his eyes.

I want that.

I've always wanted that.

I've never been the sole focus of a man before. No one's ever looked at me like I hung the moon like this guy is.

Feeling eyes on me, I sweep mine around until they land on Ben's through the glass of The Whiskey Room's windows. He's still far away, but I feel them as if he were right in front of me, and I wish I knew what he was thinking.

Turning off all the fire pits, I signal to the couple that they have five more minutes, then head inside to where Ben is. I can't keep ignoring him. I don't want things to be awkward for the rest of my time here, but it'll be hard to play it cool when all that's on my mind is climbing him like a tree.

I give him a small smile when I walk inside. "The staff is cleaning up in the tasting room and I took care of everything outside."

"What about them?" He lifts his chin to the skaters.

"I told them they have five more minutes. They look like they're having a good time and I didn't want to force them off just yet."

"That's fine. I'm still doing paperwork."

"I'm going to head off then. I just hope the roads have been plowed. I don't have four-wheel drive."

His brows come together. "You don't? How do you drive in the winter?"

"I manage just fine in the city."

"Of course." He nods, but his tone is condescending, as if it explains everything.

"What's that supposed to mean?" I ask a little too defensively. I guess my exhaustion and hunger has made me a little cranky.

"Nothing. Just that you're a city girl."

"And you're saying this is the country?"

"No. But it's definitely not city life. You can't walk to what you need, and there's a lot of long stretches of road to plow. It takes time."

"Really?" I chew on my bottom lip.

"It'll be fine. Let's go look."

"Oh, you don't have to. I'll just go myself. You said you were busy."

"Not that busy."

My heart does a little stutter in my chest, but I ignore it. At least, I try to. It's kind of hard when the man responsible for the irregular beat is walking right beside me.

But my heart completely stops when I walk out the front door and see the wintery mess in front of me.

"Uh…" is all that comes out of me, not knowing what I'm supposed to do. More snow has fallen than I thought. I've had someone shoveling the back patio every half hour, and I didn't have a view of the front lot or main road, so I had no idea.

"I can't drive in this," I say more to myself than Ben, but he runs a hand through his hair and offers up a solution.

"I have a truck. I'll take you. I just have a few things to finish up first."

"You don't have to do that."

"What are you going to do? Drive and get stuck somewhere? Walk? Sleep here? I'm not letting you."

"How nice of you," I say, my words dripping with sarcasm.

"Yes, how nice of me to not want you to freeze to death or sleep on the floor or in a chair. Besides, we're closed tomorrow, so no one will be here to unlock the refrigerator or freezer and then you'll starve."

"Fine, you can drive me back to the inn," I concede, following him back inside, secretly loving his concern for me. "I'll wait here for you to be done."

"No, you won't, let's go." He shoves his hands in his pockets and nods his head in the direction of the employees only small hallway beside the bar that leads to the distillery.

"Go where?"

"To my office."

"So I can watch you work?"

Shaking his head, I can see him fighting a smile. "Do you have to fight me on everything?"

"When it comes to you, yes."

Sighing, he scrubs his hands down his face. "How about I get you a glass of wine? I just don't want you waiting down here by yourself. I'll only be another twenty minutes."

"Fine. But I want the good stuff."

Smirking, Ben walks behind the bar and pulls a glass down from the rack. "All my stuff is good stuff."

I can see that, I think to myself, eyeing him from behind.

With a glass of wine in hand, I follow Ben up to his office and sit in the chair in front of his desk. I take a long sip, needing it while I'm in the same space as him.

His office smells like him. Like soap and pine. And the thought of crawling onto his lap and burying my face in his neck pushes its way to the front of my mind, but I swallow the urge down with another gulp of wine.

"So, you like it?" he asks, and my eyes widen, thinking I accidently said my thoughts out loud.

"What?"

"The wine."

"Oh, right, the wine," I say dumbly. "Yes, I do."

"It's one of our best. This year's special, limited-edition batch."

"What makes it special?"

"We blended two of our best grape varietals and then barrel aged it for five years."

"Well, I'm not an expert, but it's really good."

"I'm glad you like it." I can hear the ring of pride in his voice and I find it really endearing. "It was the first wine I made here as the owner. I wanted something to commemorate that."

"Oh, wow." I look down at the dark red liquid. "It is special, then. And definitely commemorates that you know what you're doing."

"Thank you." I would think he's used to praise by now in his life, but I can see he's kind of shy about it, and it makes me want to crawl onto his lap even more than before.

I seriously need to keep it together before I make a fool of myself.

While Ben signs some papers and does a little work on his computer, I pull out my laptop and compile an email to send to Violet, giving her a summary of the first weekend. Just as I'm hitting send, Ben stretches back in his chair, and my eyes go to the sliver of his stomach exposed with the lift of his sweater.

My mouth goes dry.

Reaching for my glass of wine, I knock back the rest of it, wishing it wasn't going straight to my head with no food in my stomach.

I clear my throat. "Are you almost done?"

"Just finished."

"Good." Shoving my laptop in my bag, I stand and sling it over my shoulder. "I'm starving. I haven't eaten all day."

"Why not?" he asks angrily, his eyes boring into mine.

"We were busy." I shrug. "No time."

"You should've told me, or anyone, and we would've brought you food or taken over for you so you could have a break."

I stare at him with disbelief. "You would've come and taken over for me? You would've greeted people?"

"Well, no." He scratches the back of his neck. "I would've gotten someone else to do it."

"Because you're not very welcoming," I tease, suppressing a grin.

"No, I guess not," he says, stacking the papers he was signing and slipping them into a manilla folder. "Anyway"–he clears his throat–"let's get out of here."

Heading downstairs with him, he turns out the lights and locks all of the doors as we go. Outside, I can barely see my white car with how much snow has fallen.

Ben has a cover on the bed of his truck, and opening the back gate, he pulls out a long snow brush, getting to work. He clears his door off so he can start the engine, then comes around and does the same to the passenger door, opening it for me. He waits for me to climb up inside so he can close it himself, then finishes the rest of his truck.

Rubbing my hands together to try and warm them up, I watch Ben work through the window. He's fast and efficient, and when he climbs in behind the wheel, the large cab of the truck suddenly shrinks with how close we are.

He blasts the heat and I place my hands closer to the vent. "Are you sure you'll be able to make it into town?" I ask, worried, as he backs out of his parking spot, the tires crunching over the snow and sputtering just the slightest.

He looks over at me and then back to the road, skeptical. "I don't think so."

"What am I going to do?" I whisper to myself, chewing on my bottom lip.

"I won't let anything happen to you and I'm not going to leave you stranded somewhere."

"Then where am I going to sleep tonight?"

"With me," he says simply, and my head whips around to stare wide-eyed at him.

"Excuse me?" My mouth has gone bone-dry while my pulse has decided to beat to a rhythm that has my ears ringing, thinking I heard him wrong, but so hoping I didn't.

"Not *with* me, but with me," he tries to correct. "I mean, you're coming home with me."

"Ben…"

"Jesus," he grunts, rubbing his jaw. "I didn't mean it like that. I live just down the road and I have a spare room you can sleep in tonight."

"You can't be serious."

"Why not?"

"Because I… Because you are…" I can't even finish what I want to say because it would come out as an admission to something I don't want him to know.

"I'm what?"

I shake my head. "Nothing. Never mind. Fine. I appreciate the offer."

Ben drives slow down the road, the snow semi-packed down already from other drivers, but it's still falling steadily in big, cotton ball flakes.

About a half-mile down the road, he turns onto a tree-lined driveway, the tires sliding slightly on the unplowed terrain. The drive is long, his house set in off the road for privacy, but I can still see it through the trees, and I'm blown away. It's huge. The front façade is made of white washed brick with two columns holding up the entryway. Large trees flank the sides of the house, and with the bare branches covered in snow, it's all so beautiful.

"This is your house? It's beautiful."

He clears his throat. "Thank you."

As we get closer, Ben presses a button on a device clipped to his sun visor, and one of the garage doors opens. He pulls right in, and the silence in the cab is deafening.

Needing air, I hop out quickly, eyeing a fancy sports car parked on the other side of the large space. I look back at Ben. It doesn't exactly scream *him*.

"Nice car."

"I don't take her out much. Too flashy for me now." Ben barely looks at the car, as if the sight of it is just a reminder of a past life he doesn't want to remember.

"I bet she's fun on a warm summer day with her top down." I run a single finger over the candy apple red curved body of the car.

When he doesn't answer me, I look over my shoulder and find his heated eyes perusing the curves of my body.

Oh.

Oh, my God.

My cheeks heat and I pop my hand on my hip. "I meant the car."

"I know," he says huskily, his eyes dark, like he was actually picturing *me* with my top down, riding shotgun in this car. Honestly, I wouldn't object to that if I knew no one would see me. I want to know what those eyes of his would look like running down my body with nothing between us.

Whoa, okay, I need to rein it in. I can't be thinking these things when I'm about to stay the night at his house.

Shoving my hands in my coat pockets, I walk back over to him. "So, I wasn't kidding when I said I hadn't eaten all day."

"I'm going to fix that." Opening the door that leads into his house, I follow behind him and let myself appreciate the view. Ben Breaker knows how to fill out a pair of jeans.

He hangs his coat on a hook in the mud/laundry room, and I follow suit. Through there, we walk into his big, beautiful kitchen with a surprisingly warm and homey feeling. Dark wood cabinets are offset with light beige walls and sand and white marble countertops.

He nods to the stools around the island. "Have a seat. I hope leftovers are okay. I made baked ziti last night."

"You cook?"

"It relaxes me."

"I feel the same about baking. I don't have much time for it, but when I do, it's like nothing else is going on. It clears my mind."

He pulls out a casserole dish from the fridge and pops it in the oven. "Do you have a specialty?"

"I don't know about specialty, but I'm known in my family for my cookies. Whenever we get together for a holiday, or if I'm just going home for a visit, I try out a new recipe to bring with me. Last month for Christmas I made double chocolate chunk peppermint pretzel cookies." I laugh at the look on his face. "I know they sound crazy, but they were really good."

"I have no doubt. I'd like to try one."

"We'll see if you earn my cookies. I don't just give them

to anyone."

Ben's eyes turn molten and his tongue peeks out to wet his bottom lip. My lungs constrict at the sight, my heart taking off double-time.

I really need to think before I speak around Ben, because apparently I want everything to come out sounding dirty. "I meant—"

"I know what you meant," he says, his eyes saying so much more, though. They're saying that his mind went right to the dirty double meaning, too.

That side of him, the one that looks at me like this, that's the one that makes me forget the other side of him. The one that is distant and closed-off, and for a lack of a better description, rude.

I've always given people the benefit of the doubt, and Ben isn't an exception to that. I know there's more to him under that gruff exterior, and despite my better judgement, I want to be the one he lets in. I want to be the one he's different with.

I shouldn't want that, but I do.

I'm leaving in two weeks to go back to Toronto. It's less than two hours away, but it's still distance, and I'm always busy. If anything were to happen between Ben and me, it would have to remain here. Like Vegas – what happens in Niagara-on-the-Lake, stays in Niagara-on-the-Lake.

When he finally looks away, I let out a breath I didn't even know I was holding.

"Would you like a glass of wine?"

"Yes, thank you. It's been a long week."

"Sorry about that," he apologizes, and I scrunch my nose.

"Why? It has nothing to do with you." Which is only semi-true. Having him on my mind all the time has been exhausting. "I just wasn't expecting this job, and I like to be prepared before an event. I didn't have much time for that and so it's been taxing."

Ben pulls down two glasses from his cabinet and pours us each a glass of wine from an open bottle on the counter.

"Thank you," he says, but the words come out rough, like they aren't ones he's used to saying.

"For what?"

"Taking over for Janet like you have. You and I both know I had my doubts about you when you arrived," he starts, and I laugh. "But you proved me wrong, and I respect that. So, thank you."

I smile. "For proving you wrong?"

"Amongst other things." He shrugs. "But mostly for the way you care about my winery."

"In that case, you're welcome. I really do care. It's not just the job for me."

"I can tell. So, it's going to take about a half-hour to heat up, do you want to go sit in the living room?"

"Sure." I follow him out of the kitchen and take a seat on his oversized couch. "Okay," I sigh, taking a sip of wine and leaning back into the cushions, "I think this is the most comfortable couch I've ever sat on."

"I'm glad you think so. I chose it for that exact reason. I fall asleep here too often."

"If I closed my eyes, I could too. But then I would miss out on your baked ziti and my stomach would hate me if I deprived it of it."

His smile spreads easy across his face. "We wouldn't want that."

"No, you wouldn't. Because when I'm hungry, I can get cranky."

"Good to know. I'll make sure you're always fed, then." He laughs, and his teasing tone has my mind thinking about more than just food.

God, why do I keep taking everything we say and make it dirty?

Staying with him tonight is definitely not going to help in stopping that, either. Especially when I know he'll be naked at some point behind closed doors, and I pray to the big man upstairs that I don't get a peek. Because if I do, then all bets are off and I'm going to toss all of my common sense out the window and throw myself at him. Or rather, on top of him.

"That would be wise," I tell him, continuing to sip my wine.

Ben turns on the TV. "What do you want to watch?"

"Anything is fine. I'm easy."

Oh. My. God.

What the hell is wrong with me?

My eyes dart to the side and I see Ben's sexy little smirk he's keeping to himself. Thankfully, he lets my comment go without one of his own.

"Do you like New Girl?" he asks passively, but I turn to him with my mouth hanging open.

"Are you serious? It's one of my favorite shows. You like New Girl?"

"Is that weird?"

"Well, I had you pegged as more of a Real Housewives and Kardashians man." I shrug, and he cringes, making me laugh. "I'm glad to be wrong. Can we start with the fourth season? I think it's the funniest one."

His eyes flare. "So do I."

Unzipping my heeled boots, I place them beside the couch and tuck my feet up under me, feeling relaxed for the first time in a long while. Ben's presence has made me feel uncomfortable, nervous, small, and hot and bothered in an array of ways this past week. But right now, here in his home with him, I'm feeling relaxed and comfortable.

Sitting on opposite ends of his couch, we eat big bowls of baked ziti with extra mozzarella while finishing off the bottle of wine and watching New Girl. Hearing him chuckle at the same parts as me has me biting my lip, loving that he has a sense of humor buried somewhere in there.

At some point though, I can't hold off anymore, and I yawn. Covering my mouth, I place my feet on the soft rug. "If you don't mind, I think I'll go to bed."

"I'll show you where you'll be." He turns off the TV and I follow him upstairs, my eyes staying glued to his firm ass the entire way. "This'll be your room for the night. I hope it's okay."

I step inside and smile, turning to face him. "It's great, thank you. But I, uh…" I nervously tuck a piece of hair behind my ear. "I don't have anything to change into, and I really don't want to sleep in this." His eyes run down my body, the oversized sweater and jeans I'm wearing suddenly feeling too tight.

He clears his throat. "I'll find you something." Ben leaves without another word and returns a minute later holding a t-shirt and sweatpants. "They might be too big."

"I'm sure it'll be fine. Thank you." Our fingers brush when I take the clothes from his hands, and a jolt of electricity zaps up my arm as if he electrocuted me. I suck in a sharp breath, my eyes flinging to his, seeing the same response in them.

He felt it too.

"Goodnight, Leah."

I swallow hard, the rough whisper of his voice turning my insides to putty. "Goodnight," I manage to get out past my tight throat.

He backs out of the room but keeps his eyes on me, pausing in the doorway. "The bathroom is across the hall."

I nod and he closes the door, but I remain standing where I am, unable to move just yet. When I finally can, I strip out of my clothes and slip into his sweatpants and t-shirt. The soft fabrics feel like they've been washed over and over, and I bite my lip, thinking about him wearing them.

And with those thoughts, I slide between the sheets, sleep now the furthest thing from my mind.

Chapter 7

I can't get to sleep no matter how hard I try. I've been staring at the ceiling for over an hour and I can't get my mind to shut off thoughts of Ben and what he's doing right now.

Huffing out a lungful of air, I throw the covers off and swing my legs over the side, running my hands through my hair. Standing, I pace the room for a minute before gaining the courage to open the bedroom door. I look to the left and right, then sneak across the hall to use the bathroom before tiptoeing downstairs to the kitchen.

I open a few cabinets until I find where he keeps the glasses, and I fill one with filtered water from the refrigerator door.

"Couldn't sleep?"

I'm in the middle of drinking when Ben's voice scares the hell out of me. I jump, the glass slipping out of my hand and crashing at my feet.

"Shit, don't move," he instructs, and considering I'm barefoot, I'm inclined to listen. "I didn't mean to scare you."

"It's okay."

Coming up next to me, glass crunches under his moccasin slippers. "I'm going to lift you up onto the counter," he warns, just as his hands come to rest on my hips. "Okay?"

He's so close to me. "Okay," I whisper, and his eyes dart down to my mouth and back up.

His hands tighten on my hips just before he lifts me up onto the counter beside the fridge, and he doesn't let go of me right away. He lingers, spreading his fingers out, gripping the t-shirt he gave me.

He's a big man and I'm a curvy woman, so his clothes fit me just fine. I'm sure he's used to women who his clothes would hang off of, and maybe even be able to wear just the shirt as a dress, but that's not me. That'll never be me, and I'm more than okay with that. And by the way Ben's looking at me, he doesn't seem to mind that I fill out his clothes the way I do. In fact, with the way he's looking at me, I know he doesn't mind.

"Let me clean this up."

I can only manage a small nod in response, never taking my eyes off of him while he squats down to pick up the bigger pieces of glass first, and then sweeps up the rest.

Grabbing another glass, he fills it with water and hands it

to me. "Thank you. I thought a glass of water might help me sleep. I guess I have too much on my mind."

"Me too," he admits, his eyes holding mine. "Do you think ice cream would help?"

"Well, there's only one way to find out." I smile, and he pulls out a carton of vanilla peanut butter swirl from the freezer. "I love anything peanut butter," I confess.

"Noted." He nods, scooping out a bowl for each of us. "Want to watch some more New Girl?"

"That's always a yes."

Kicking off his slippers, he places them on my feet. "They're big, but just in case I missed any glass, you'll be protected."

"What about you?"

"I'll be fine."

"Such a gentleman."

"I haven't been called that..." He pauses, looking up at the ceiling. "Well, ever."

I flash him a smile. "You have your moments."

Ben holds his hand out for me and I place mine in his, the large size and warmth enveloping mine. Hopping down from the counter, I go to take my hand out of his, but he hesitates, not letting go right away.

I roll my lips between my teeth, holding back my grin as I follow Ben into the living room. I take my place on the couch like before, but instead of Ben sitting at the other end, he takes the spot right beside me, handing me my bowl of ice cream. "I also have peanut butter whiskey if you think it'll help."

I perk up. "Peanut butter whiskey? I'm intrigued."

Ben gets up and comes back a minute later with two tumblers of whiskey, handing me one.

I sniff the amber liquid and my eyes widen. "Oh, wow, it smells like peanut butter!" I say excitedly, and when I take a tentative sip, I'm even more surprised. "Holy sh–" I cut myself off, "that's amazing. Not too much. Just enough of a hint of peanut butter without being overbearing."

"I'm glad you like it."

"I'm still holding you to that tasting at the distillery. I've always been a wine girl, but I like the way whiskey feels as it spreads through me."

Ben eyes me over the rim of his glass and my eyes drop to his throat working around a swallow. Every move he makes has me enthralled, and he's not even trying. He's just…being. And that's why he's so dangerous to me.

"You could be both," he offers. "A whiskey and wine girl is an interesting one. Strong and sweet – a lethal combination."

"I like the way that sounds," I tell him, taking another sip of whiskey. I place it on the coffee table and start in on my ice cream, the two peanut butter flavors mixing and dancing in my mouth. "More New Girl, please," I direct, waving my spoon at the TV.

I catch his smile before he shoves a spoonful of ice cream into his mouth and presses play. I wish I could tear my eyes away from his mouth, but then his tongue makes an appearance around the spoon, and the whiskey flowing through me goes straight to my head while the rest of me aches for him.

I force my eyes closed and take a deep breath, trying to calm my heart. This man is going to keep me up all night with thoughts of his tongue doing wicked things to me while licking melted ice cream from my body.

Shoving another spoonful into my mouth, I pray I don't do something stupid like actually ask him to do just that.

"How did you get into the event business?" he asks casually, and I'm grateful for the distraction.

"My aunt is actually Violet of Violet's Designs."

"Really?"

"Yeah." I nod. "I'm from a small town in New York, and every summer in high school and college, I would stay with her and work for her."

"You two must be close then."

"I don't know about *close*." I shrug. "She never lets me call her 'aunt' at work, which I don't really mind, because I don't want anyone thinking I get special treatment. She's a very private person and tends to choose her company and career over everything else. So, we're close in that we work together and respect each other, but we don't hang out or go places together outside of work."

"Do you wish you were closer?"

"I do," I admit. "The rest of my family is in New York and I don't have many friends. I mostly just work." Jesus, my life sounds pathetic. "I don't want to become her," I whisper, confessing that out loud for the first time. I've wanted to be like her with her career, but I don't want to become her.

"You don't have to."

"It's easier said than done. I'm basically on the same track as her." Finishing my ice cream, I trade my empty bowl for my glass of whiskey and lean back against the couch, rolling my head to the side to look at Ben.

"You could always hop off the train. Or, take control of it and switch tracks. Or even derail that shit if you want. It's always what *you* want, Leah. *Your* life is whatever *you* want it to be."

"Is yours?"

"Yes," he says with all seriousness. "I've had to adapt to changes out of my control, but I've still made all the choices that have led me here."

"What do you mean?"

"I had one too many concussions and was told if I didn't stop playing hockey, then the next time I might suffer irreversible damage. I had a choice to make. It was an easy one to make, but a hard one to accept. Playing hockey was all I wanted in life, and without it, I had to figure out who I was and who I would be."

"How did you do that?"

"I just started with the fact that I wanted to live long enough to find out. The rest came when my parents wanted to slow down and retire. So, I bought them out."

"Do you love it, though? Or were you just doing your parents a favor?"

"I loved the winery growing up. I would run through the vines and hide for hours, pretending I was battling some unknown enemy." Ben's eyes take on a faraway look, lost in his memories. "But as I got older, and more into sports and girls"—he smirks—"I stopped spending time there. Buying it from them and being there again has given me a newfound purpose and has reminded me how much I loved it. It's my family's legacy."

"And now yours," I tell him. "You put your own stamp on the place by expanding it."

"My parents always wanted to do more but didn't think it was worth it when so close to retirement and not knowing what my plans were after I eventually retired. Turns out that was decided for me earlier than I thought."

"You're okay though, right?" I ask tentatively, worried.

"I am," he says softly, his eyes holding mine. "I just can't take any hard hits. So, don't get any ideas the next time I'm an asshole." The corners of his mouth lift in a small smile that I return.

"I would never. But just to be sure, maybe you should try to not be an asshole to me anymore."

"Just you?"

"Start with me." I laugh lightly. "Then we'll work on everyone else."

"I really am sorry, Leah," he says, and I sober.

"Thank you," I whisper. "I appreciate that. And I appreciate you letting me stay with you. I didn't really like the idea of being stranded on the side of the road to turn into a popsicle."

"I didn't either."

I pause, wanting to bring something up, but not knowing how he'll react. "I looked you up, you know. Before my first day."

"And what did you find?" His voice is strained, already knowing what I found.

"Pictures of you. You seemed different back when you were playing hockey. Happy."

"I was." He pauses. "Until I wasn't."

"What changed? Your concussions?"

"Yes and no."

"You don't have talk about it if you don't want to. I shouldn't have brought it up. Do you mind if I have a refill?" I hold my empty glass out and he takes it, refilling both of our glasses.

"It's not that I don't want to," he says when he sits back down beside me. "It's just that I haven't talked about it before. To anyone."

"Why not?"

"Because I don't trust anyone anymore."

"Ben..." I trail off, not expecting him to say that.

He takes a deep breath and lets it out in a rush, looking up at the ceiling. I wait for him to say more, not wanting to pressure him, but I want to know everything.

"I loved everything about the life I was living. I got paid an exorbitant amount of money to wake up every day and play the sport I love. I had fans, women throwing themselves at me...it was every man's dream."

"I'll bet," I say bitterly, tasting acid on my tongue.

"I learned the harsh truths of these women, though." The hardness in his tone makes me believe it wasn't actually every man's dream. "Turns out every man's dream is just a twisted nightmare with a beautiful face."

"What changed?"

"You said you looked me up," he clips, rubbing his jaw. "You saw the articles."

"I did, but they were tabloid articles. I'd rather hear the truth from you."

His eyes find mine, studying me before answering. "I was dating this girl for a while. I met her at a bar after a game. The place was known as a local spot we went to after home games, which meant it was also filled with puck bunnies looking to get noticed. That should've been the first red flag."

"Puck bunnies?" I interrupt, unable to hold back. "Are you serious? That's a thing?"

"Yeah." He shrugs. "It's just a part of the life – women after you for money and fame. Same bullshit all pro-athletes deal with."

"But you thought she was different?"

"I did." He nods, taking a long drink of whiskey. "Things moved pretty quick. She said and did all the right things to make me trust her. To make me fall in love with her. But it was all just a lie and a ploy to get her claim to fame and a paycheck to match. You read what she said about me." His eyes dart to mine and I can see the embarrassment in them – the shame. "Do you believe what she said?" he asks carefully, and I can tell my answer is important to him. "Do you think I treated her like that?" His jaw clenches, unable to say the details.

"No, Ben, I don't," I tell him, and his shoulders visibly sag in relief. I might have at first, but after this week, I don't believe he's that kind of guy. Even when he's an asshole, he's not evil. "Why did she say those things?"

"It was right after I announced that I was retiring. I got another concussion in our last game of the season and the doctor laid it all out for me. I talked to my coaches and the owner, and I was able to get out of my last year I still had contracted."

"But you didn't tell her?"

He shakes head. "I only told my family and the few close friends I had the truth. I didn't want to have to justify myself, or justify needing to prioritize myself over the fans and team."

"And you shouldn't have to. You still don't." I reach out and place my hand on his arm and he looks down at where I'm touching him, then into my eyes.

I see the pain he tries to hide seeping out, and despite everything that's happened since meeting him, I want to take his pain away. I want to be the balm that soothes his lonely heart. I want to be the one he trusts again after all these years.

"The people who matter know the truth, yes?" I ask, and he nods, his eyes darting between mine. "Then everyone else can fuck off, yes?"

Smirking, Ben nods again. "Yes. I never got to tell her, though. I was still processing everything for myself when she went and sold out her story to the highest bidder. She faked pictures around my house to go with it, too. I guess she realized her life in the spotlight, traveling with me to games, and hanging out with the other hockey girlfriends was all over. Being with me was never about love."

"Ben…"

"I suddenly had this...*thing* hanging over my head. I was already noticing changes in myself that I didn't like and I hated that I couldn't control them. I still can't."

"What do you mean?"

"You might have noticed my..."–he tilts his head to the side–"tendency to get mad easily or be short-tempered. I don't mean or want to be, and I never really was before. It's why I don't like being around people anymore. I don't want to put myself in situations where I'm not myself."

"But you were known as Ben 'The Bone' Breaker. Wasn't a temper a part of your job on the ice?"

"It was. But that was on the ice. It was my job to protect my team, and I did my job well. Off the ice, though...that wasn't who I was. I wasn't some hot-head looking for a fight. But now...I don't know. I'm a little more like that than I'd like to be. Working helps. Being there gives me focus and purpose."

"I get that," I tell him. "But I think you need something outside of work. No one can predict the future. You shouldn't miss out on all the joys of life because of fear." Ben's face shuts down and I immediately know my mistake. "I'm sorry. I shouldn't have said that."

"No, it's fine. You're just speaking your mind."

"But I have no right to give you advice when I don't even follow it myself. All I do is work, too," I admit, swirling the whiskey in my glass. "I've been on a one-track path since I was fifteen, not caring much for anything that would derail me from that path. And spending every summer with my aunt in another country away from my friends meant I missed out on a lot. While they bonded over new experiences and boys, I was learning about floral arrangements, tablescapes, the perfect food pairings, wine, blah, blah, blah."

"Blah, blah, blah?" He grins. "Did it not interest you?"

"Of course it did. Or does. But sometimes I wonder, like now, if it was worth missing out on years I can never get back. I try not to dwell on it because I love what I do, but you can't go back and be young again."

"You also can't beat yourself up on decisions you made in the past that you wanted at the time. We all wish we could know the answers to 'what if' or go back and make a different choice on any number of things in our past. But the truth is, we once wanted what we decided. The only thing that has changed is that we're older and have perspective to know better now."

I take a moment to think over what he just said. "I never thought of it that way. But you're absolutely right."

"I could get used to hearing that." He jokes, his smile coming easy, making my stomach knot.

"I'm sure you could. But don't hold your breath." I laugh.

Sipping my drink, I close my eyes briefly, only to open them and find Ben's on me, studying me, a look on his face. "What?" I whisper, my throat closing. The desire in his eyes is making me wish I could crawl onto his lap and kiss him. I want to taste the peanut butter whiskey on his lips.

He reaches out and tucks a strand of hair behind my ear. When his fingers brush my cheek, my skin heats, and I feel his touch travel through me, all the way to my toes.

As much as I want to lean into his touch, I resist, choosing to take a sip of whiskey to try and hide my reaction. It has the opposite effect of what I want, though, and instead amplifies my desire for more of his touch.

"Ben…" His name is rough coming from my tight throat. "We, uhm… I can't…" I try and get out that we can't do this, but I don't want to say it. Mostly because I want to go there with him. I just don't want to say it out loud.

"Whatever you say," he rasps, his voice rough too, which only makes me want to feel it against my skin while he kisses his way down my body and whispers the dirty things he's going to do to me.

He lingers for a long moment before dropping his hand back down to the couch.

His eyes are on the TV, but the air between us is different now. Charged. And it takes everything in me to ignore it and stick to the couch cushion I'm on.

Finishing off the amber liquid in my glass, I curl my feet up next to me, my eyes eventually falling closed.

They flutter open again when I'm moved, but I'm too comfortable to care. When I'm jostled further, I peel my eyes open to see why, and instead of seeing his living room and TV, I'm eye level with a broad chest.

What the…?

This can't be real. Is Ben carrying me upstairs?

I reach up to touch his chiseled jawline covered in stubble and Ben's eyes find mine in an instant, his face coming into full view.

"Am I dreaming?" I whisper, and the arms banded

around me tighten.

"No, Leah, you're not." I feel the vibrations of his words travel through his chest and right into me, and I lower my hand to rest there in the middle of his chest, wanting to feel it again.

"You didn't have to carry me. I'm probably too heavy."

I didn't mean it in a self-deprecating way, more of it being a plain fact, but Ben's face twists in confusion. "You're not heavy, Leah," he says with complete seriousness, and I smile at the feel of his voice again. "You're perfect," he adds, his face soft and open.

He thinks I'm perfect.

This gorgeous man finds me perfect.

I would question it if I weren't still half-asleep, but I am, and I like the way it makes my chest warm too much.

"You too," I say without thought, and he chuckles, shaking me in his arms. "I mean," I try and coverup, but he silences me with a shake of his head.

"Nope. You can't take it back. You think I'm perfect, too." He's teasing me, and I hide my smile against his chest, loving this playful side of him.

Ben gently lays me down in bed and pulls the covers over me. "Sleep well, Leah," he whispers, his fingers gently brushing the hair away from my face.

"'Night," I manage to say around a yawn, my eyes already closed again.

Chapter 8

The morning light streams in through the windows and I turn over, burying my face in the pillows. Groaning, I roll onto my back and rub my eyes, but smile when I remember that Ben really did carry me up here last night. I really was tucked against his hard chest like Lois Lane in Superman's arms. And I wasn't too heavy for him.

He's strong enough to handle me like I weigh nothing at all, and that's never happened before. It makes me think of all the ways he could pick me up and throw me around, taking from me what he wants and using me however he pleases.

My skin tingles, down my back and legs, wishing he would.

Rubbing my thighs together, I try and calm the throbbing between them, but it doesn't work.

I can't ignore it, and I certainly can't face Ben like this.

Closing my eyes, I let Ben's face filter in behind my lids – him smiling, him with that little crooked smirk, him annoyed, him laughing. Every aspect of him I've seen and met flashes behind my lids and I slide my hands down my body, slipping one beneath the waistband of his sweatpants, wishing it was him covering me and not just his clothes.

I only have my fingers to work with right now, but with how tightly wound I feel, it's enough. Ben's already taken care of that. And when I slip my hand inside my panties, I find myself wetter than I've ever been with just the thought of being with him.

Biting my lip, I hold back a moan while I circle my clit, the first pass feeling like a live wire shock straight through me.

I slide my other hand back up my body and under his t-shirt to cup my breast, circling my nipple with the tip of my finger.

Oh, God.

Rolling it between my thumb and forefinger, I press down on my clit and a whimper escapes my tightly pressed lips.

Shit.

Rolling onto my stomach, I bury my face in a pillow and continue to work my clit, needing this release more than anything. My mind goes to a place where Ben is picking me up and pressing me against the wall, his hard body, hot mouth, and eager hands all over me.

Grunting at the images playing behind my lids, I slip two fingers inside of myself and rub my clit harder.

Fuuucckkk.

Exploding around my fingers, my long and low groan is absorbed by the pillows, and when I come down from the high of my release, my body feels boneless and I'm panting.

I can't move yet.

I can't open my eyes yet.

All I can do is lie here.

I haven't had an orgasm like that in…I don't know. And that's truly sad. One, because it was me giving it to myself, and two, because my ex never gave me one like that no matter what we were doing. All it took was thinking about Ben, and if just thinking about him brings me the best orgasm of my life, I can't imagine what having him actually with me and inside of me would bring me.

Damn it. I'm working myself up again.

Kicking off the covers, I push my messy hair from my face and make a dash for the bathroom across the hall. Noticing the flush to my cheeks, I throw my hair up into a bun and take a quick shower to cool off, then put Ben's clothes back on. Minus my panties this time, I feel like I'm hiding a dirty little secret I wish I could share, but know it'd only bring trouble.

I don't hear any movement to indicate that Ben's anywhere up here, and making my way downstairs, I still don't hear—

Wait, what's that sound?

I walk quietly around the first level of his home, and it isn't until I get into the kitchen that I hear it again. Like metal clinking? Was that a grunt?

Walking through the mud room to the garage door that's open maybe six inches, I hold my breath, nervous for what I might find. But nothing prepares me for the sight of Ben working out.

Holy. Mother. Of. All. Things.

Ben is shirtless.

His back is to me and my eyes have the opportunity to take him in fully. His gym shorts are sitting low on his hips and I watch as his muscles flex and bunch, glistening under a sheen of sweat as he lifts weights.

I'm light-headed.

The little bursts of air he releases with every curl of his arms has my core throbbing. I feel myself getting slick with need again and I clench my thighs together, wishing I could see those sexy arms flex on either side of my head as he thrusts into me.

All that power.

All that pent-up emotion he never expresses…

I want it all to be unleashed on me.

His face could make angels weep, but his body could make even the most holy fall to their knees, praying for a taste.

I don't know how long I stand here, hidden beside the doorframe watching him, but I can't look away. When he finishes his set, he grabs a towel and wipes his face and chest, and I know I should look away. I should walk back into the kitchen and stick my head in the freezer and remember that Ben Breaker is a client. But hell, my lady parts are screaming that it wouldn't matter if he were a serial killer, let alone a client. I want him.

As if in slow motion, Ben rubs the towel over his sweat drenched hair, shaking it out, turning towards me.

I still don't move.

In fact, I want him to see me watching him. I want to know what he'll do – what he'll say.

He takes two steps forward and lifts his eyes, meeting mine. He doesn't falter in his strides, as if he already knew I was there and was putting on a show. And if I could, I'd buy every damn available ticket to that show so no one else got to see it.

"Good morning, Leah." Those three words. That's it. Those three words have me licking my lips. Yes, it is a good morning.

"Morning," I manage to get out despite my mouth being bone-dry. "I, uh, didn't mean to interrupt your workout."

"You didn't?" Ben takes the two stairs up to me and pushes the door open, forcing me to back up until I hit the wall.

He's so close.

He's crowding my space, and when I get a whiff of his manly sweat, my dry mouth waters.

I never thought that I'd find the scent of sweat so sexy, but I have the desire to lick him from the waist of his shorts, up his abs and chest, the column of his neck, then across the line of his jaw before finally tasting his lips.

Ben tosses the towel he's holding onto the washing machine. "Because I knew the moment you started watching me."

My pulse is racing. "You did?"

"Yes."

"I...sorry?"

"Are you?" he taunts, his little smirk making my heart flutter.

"No." The word leaves my mouth before I can stop it, which only makes his smirk grow.

"Are you hungry?"

"Y-yes." Shit. "You mean for, uhm, breakfast?"

"What else would I be talking about?"

You.

I clear my throat. "I don't know."

"How do pancakes sound?"

Like the second-best thing I could put in my mouth right now, I think. Alright, my mind has just overflowed from the gutter and plummeted to the pit of mud beneath.

"Really good." Was that too breathy? Do I sound as turned on as I feel?

Ben runs his hand through his damp hair and leaves me panting against the wall while he swaggers into the kitchen.

I take a moment to regroup and get my mind back to a safe place where I'm not about to drop to my knees and beg him to let me have a taste.

"Coffee?" he asks, looking over his shoulder at me when I finally make my way into the kitchen.

"Please." I nod, and he pours me a mug, placing it in

front of me. "Thanks."

Ben doesn't change or shower before getting to work on breakfast, and I'm grateful for the extended view. I can't take my eyes off of him. Something seems different this morning with him, and I really wish that orgasm I gave myself earlier was enough to satisfy me, but it wasn't. I know if I slipped my hand between my legs right now, it would only take the smallest of touches to make me come again.

"It stopped snowing an hour ago and I have a crew coming to work on the winery's parking lot. They're going to dig your car out and clear it off. I can take you over there when it's done." Ben places a stack of pancakes in front of me, along with butter and syrup.

"Okay." I have a hard time looking him in the face when his bare chest is in my sightline.

I cut into my stack and close my eyes, a soft moan leaving me. "I think these are the best pancakes I've ever had," I mumble around my bite.

Opening my eyes, I find his have gone dark, boring into mine.

"Thank you. It's my family's secret recipe."

"You should never tell anyone," I say as I shove another forkful into my mouth. "Because this is like crack and you'd have the whole world addicted."

"We wouldn't want that, would we?" he teases.

"No, because I think I already am and I don't want the competition," I tell him, and he winks.

"That was the plan."

I swallow hard. "To get me addicted?" I whisper.

He doesn't answer me right away, and instead makes his own stack of pancakes and sits down at a stool across from me.

His eyes lift to mine. "Eat."

"Avoiding the question, I see." Smiling, I slide the fork between my lips to lick off the excess syrup and his eyes zero in on my mouth, watching my every move.

"Not avoiding. I'm choosing not to answer because I don't think you're ready for it."

My chest constricts. "What makes you think that?"

With a devilish little smirk, Ben takes a drink of coffee, his eyes never leaving mine. What answer does he think I'm not ready for? Because I want to hear it. I want to know what he's thinking. I want whatever he wants to give me. The look in his eyes makes me think he wants to lay me out on his kitchen island and lick syrup off of me, and I'm all freaking for it. I'd return the favor in a heartbeat, too.

"Just eat, Leah."

Frustrated, I huff out a breath and scarf down the rest of my pancakes, not caring in the least that I might look like a pig shoving food in my mouth. I'm pissed off, and I'm afraid if I don't have food in my mouth, then I'll say something I'll regret.

Carrying my plate to the sink, I purposefully leave it there for him to deal with and walk right out of the kitchen and back up to the room I was in.

Just when I thought I made some headway with Ben, he goes and says something that makes me want to slap some sense into him.

Pacing the length of the room, my mind races with everything he could have said to me when he meant I wasn't ready to hear what he had to say.

He wants me addicted to him?

He wants me addicted to his food?

Because done and done. I haven't even had him yet and I'm addicted to him.

Shit.

I need to put some distance between us, and I'm not leaving this room until he says my car is dug out.

It takes a few hours, but Ben eventually knocks on the door. I'm glad he left me alone, but I was also hoping he wouldn't. I was hoping he would barge in here and show me exactly how addicted he intends I become.

I'm snuggled in bed watching a movie and I don't feel like moving, so I call out, "Come in."

He opens the door and his eyes roam down the length of me beneath the covers. "I just got a call saying the lot and your car are clear. So, whenever you're ready…" He rubs his jaw.

"Alright, just give me a few minutes."

Nodding, he closes the door again and I throw the covers off. I make the bed and then take off his sweatpants and t-shirt, leaving them folded neatly on the comforter.

Sighing, I put my clothes from yesterday back on, wishing I could wear his instead, but not really having a reason to other than my need to have a piece of him.

"Ready?" Ben asks when I enter the kitchen. He's dressed in a pair of dark jeans and a quarter-zip sweater. It's unfair how good he looks in everything he wears.

"Yes. Sure." I follow him out to the garage and into his truck.

I'm glad the roads are clear. If I had to spend another day and night with Ben, I don't know what I would've done. I already know I'm heading down a path that's only setting me up for heartache.

Even still, last night with Ben was nice. More than nice, actually. We both shared secrets and truths that neither of us had before, and it felt…real. It felt intimate. Did I want to rip his clothes off and climb him like a tree? Yes. But I also never wanted him to stop talking. The sound of his voice is like whiskey and wine. Sweet, smooth, dark, rich, and packs a punch that leaves me lightheaded and off balance.

Pulling out onto the main road, I marvel at the bare trees that are coated like powdered sugar and the roofs of houses like icing.

Music fills the truck's cab as we ride down the road to Breaker Estates, but when he parks beside my car and turns the radio down, I feel the weight of our silence.

"Thanks again for letting me stay with you." With my hand on the door handle, Ben reaches out and stops me with his hand on my forearm.

"Leah." My name rumbles from his chest

I turn back to look at him. "Yes?"

He doesn't say anything at first, just holds my attention. "I'll see you Thursday?"

"Yes. Thursday." He releases my arm and I climb out of his truck.

Taking a deep breath with my back turned to him so he doesn't see my reaction to his touch, I slide into my car and start the engine. I have to wait for it to warm up, and I'm praying Ben leaves, but he doesn't. He waits beside me for five minutes, and even follows me all the way to the inn. Only when I park does he make a U-turn in the lot and head back in the direction of his house.

Chapter 9

I spent the past two days touring a few of the wineries around the Twenty Valley and Niagara-on-the-Lake areas, sampling wine and food and taking notes. I made pro/con lists, rough sketches of the layouts of the buildings and properties, and what I would change if I could.

All in all, it was relaxing and productive. I'm not very good at relaxing and don't have much practice in it, so I thought mixing a little fun and business would help, and it did.

Some of the wineries have their vision and execution down while others could use a little guidance and rebranding. I'd love to help make Breaker Estates better than it already is, but God forbid I ever bring up a change or improvement to

Ben. He'd probably have a coronary.

With one weekend under my belt, I know what to expect now, and I don't have much prep for tomorrow besides setting up the welcome tables and arranging the vases of flowers for the tables.

I'm in the kitchen cutting the stems of flowers when Ben walks in. I know the moment he does because the air around me changes. I've never been so aware of another person like I am with Ben. I can sense when he's near and when his eyes are on me, even from a distance.

My back is to him as I put together the vases of flowers, and I hear him talk with Chef Casey about something for a brief moment before he's right there beside me.

"Leah." I close my eyes for a moment. Why does he have to say my name like that?

"Good afternoon." Good afternoon? Seriously? Is that what I just said?

"Will you be available later for me?"

My eyes flit to his and then back to my flowers. "For what?" Does he have to stand so close to me?

"I wanted to give you that whiskey tasting. You know, in case you get asked any questions from anyone."

Right, of course. Because it's not like he just wants to get tipsy and spill some more secrets with me or anything…

I wish.

"Sure. Yes. That sounds good." Do I sound nervous? Because I am. I don't know how many more times I can be alone with him and not beg him to kiss me.

I see his hand flex against the counter beside me and I

wonder if he's resisting the urge to not touch me as much as I'm wishing he would. Even just a brush of his hand down my arm would make me need to take a long break in the bathroom while I took care of myself.

"Find me later when you're done down here," he says close to my ear, sending a shiver down my spine.

Is he playing with me right now?

"Okay," I breathe, my voice not even close to being able to work.

Only when he walks away am I able to breathe regularly again and my heart settles back down to a pace that's not putting me at risk for a heart attack.

❄ ❄ ❄ ❄

I've stalled for as long as I could, but I literally have nothing left to do but go up to Ben's office.

I give Charlie a smile as I pass him in the distillery and make my way up the stairs, my palms sweating like I've been called to the principal's office.

He's just a man. He's just a man. He's just a man. I repeat the mantra in my head as if it will help.

Raising my fist, I knock lightly on the door. "Come in," he calls, like he did that first day. His eyes roam my body from head to toe when I step inside, and when they settle on mine, they're different. He's looking at me like he did when we were on his couch. There's heat, possession, need, and hunger in his eyes.

"I thought we'd wait until The Whiskey Room was

closed. I don't want anyone getting the wrong idea."

"That you spend your free time drinking in your own bar?"

"Yes, or that I do private tastings." The word 'private' rolls from his tongue like a dirty caress, and my core clenches, feeling it there as if he really did touch me.

"We wouldn't want that now, would we?" I tease.

"No, we wouldn't."

I walk over to the windows he has that overlook the vineyard and patio, smiling at the people skating. "I don't know the last time I did that," I say quietly, more to myself than him.

"Did what?"

"Ice skate. I remember loving it as a kid. The freedom of gliding along the ice as if I were floating. It felt like magic. I didn't understand how a person could balance on a thin blade like that."

"You can skate down there anytime you'd like."

"How about now?" I ask, looking back at him. "We're waiting for closing time anyhow," I add, but I can see the reluctance in his eyes. "When was the last time you skated just for fun?"

"I haven't been on the ice since my last game," he admits, running his hand through his hair.

"Really?"

"Yeah." I can hear the regret in his voice and I want to fix it.

I give him a big smile, excitement coursing through me. "Come on, then. Let's go down there together."

His smile is slow to come, but the corners of his mouth lift and he shakes his head. "Fine."

Walking downstairs, those still eating and drinking in the restaurant turn to look at us, then whisper to whoever they're with that 'it's him', while giving me questioning looks that I ignore.

Ben places his hand on my lower back and we walk outside, straight to the skate rental hut.

"Hey, Ben," the kid working behind the counter greets, a huge smile on his face.

"Hi, Kenny. How's the season looking for you?"

"We're going all the way this year," he says proudly.

"With you leading them, I know you will."

"Thanks, Ben," he says excitedly, then looks at me. "Wow, sorry for being rude. I'm Kenny."

"Leah." I grin.

"What can I get for you guys? Are you here for skates?"

"We are. I'm a size ten."

"Thirteen for me," Ben says, and I want to pass out. I don't care if people say that the size of a man's feet isn't a correlation to his penis, because everything about Ben is *big*. So I know he has to be big everywhere, right?

Kenny hands us our skates and we walk over to a bench to put them on. "You're going to make sure I don't fall, right?"

"If you make sure I don't." He smirks, making me laugh. "Seriously?"

"Yeah. It's been a while. What if I forgot?"

"I guess we'll see." Standing, I put on my gloves that

were stuffed in my pockets and hold my had out for him to take. And the moment he places his in mine, I'm sparked alive. Even through my glove, I can feel his touch.

Does he feel it too?

He said he wanted me addicted, and I'm halfway there. Correction, three quarters there. Even when he's an asshole. Now that I know his mood swings are because of a head injury, I believe he deserves some leeway. He deserves all the compassion that I know he doesn't give himself.

As I take the first step towards the ice, it's a little shaky. Walking on skates is like a baby giraffe walking for the first time. I squeeze his hand and he holds mine harder in return, letting me know he's not going to let me fall.

There are other people on the ice, but I don't notice them. I don't see anyone else. I just feel Ben's hand in mine as I grip the ledge of the rink and step onto the ice, waiting for him to join me. When he does, the look on his face changes. It's the first time he's touched the ice with skates since his last game, and the fact that he's letting me have this moment with him, stirs something in me.

"Please don't let me fall, Ben. I haven't done this in forever."

He glides right up to me, my back hitting the ledge. "I won't let anything happen to you. You're safe with me," he tells me, and every cell and fiber of my body sparks alive. I don't know any other way to explain it. "We'll take it slow. I promise."

Ben takes both my hands in his and skates backwards, pulling me along with him. A carefree laugh bubbles out of me and Ben looks down at me with a smile of his own, his blue eyes dancing.

"You're doing so good, Leah."

"You're not so bad yourself, Ben. And you were afraid you'd forgotten how to skate."

"I wasn't too worried."

He continues to pull me around the ice, and I'm so lost in the moment with him that I'm not ready for when he turns us. I mistakenly pick my skate up instead of continuing to glide right along and I get tripped up, stumbling forward into him. His arms immediately come around me, catching me.

"Oh, sorry." I laugh. "I wasn't prepared to turn." My face is even with his chest and I look up, our faces close, but still too far away with how tall he is. Everything in me is begging him to lean down and close the distance. His lips are so inviting. Everything about him is so inviting.

"I…" I stumble over my words before pushing away from him. "I think I'm ready to try on my own."

"Are you sure?"

"Just stay close in case I need you."

"Anything you want."

I skate on my own, one foot gliding, the next foot gliding. I lift my arms out to the sides and it's like when I was a kid. It's freeing and feels like I'm flying. It's like magic. Even as a grown adult, I still don't understand how I can balance on the edge of this blade at the bottom of my feet. But it's beautiful and it's something I don't want to forget or miss out on again for as many years as I have.

With my head up looking at the stars, I'm too lost in my

own space to notice that there are kids skating right towards me. Luckily, Ben is right there to pull me out of the way, but I stumble, and my skates slide out from under me.

Ben wraps his arms around me and sweeps me up, hauling me against him before I have the chance to fall on my ass. Instead, I fall against a hard chest. The same one I saw glistening in sweat just a few days ago, and the same one I wish I could lick every inch of.

My breath is knocked out of me. "Thank you," I finally manage. "I didn't see them there. I was lost in my own space."

"Yeah, I noticed. You looked like you were really enjoying yourself."

"I was."

His head dips down so our faces are closer – his lips right there for the taking. If my skates were touching the ice right now, I would push up on the toe picks and close the distance, consequences be damned. I couldn't care less at this point that he's a client. I was just fooling myself anyway, trying to resist the inevitable.

Clearing my throat, I grip his jacket in my hands. "I think it's safe for you to put me down now."

"Are you sure? I don't want you running anyone over."

"I promise I'll watch where I'm going. Or you could just pull me out of the way again."

"Gladly."

"Or..." I drag out, ready to make a bold suggestion. "You could hold my hand so I don't make any more mistakes."

"I can do that."

Despite the cold, my cheeks heat, and I feel like some hormonal teenager spending time with her crush. Ben just makes me feel all of these things that I was missing out on in life. I've dated, and I've had a couple boyfriends, but no one has ever made me giddy or made feel beautiful and seen like he does.

I'm confident with my size. I love who I am and I know who I am, and men tend to be intimidated by that. But Ben…he sees it and looks at me with this heat in his eyes like I'm everything he wants and needs.

We keep skating and he smiles, looking like he's having fun. I don't think he gets to have fun anymore. He doesn't even care that there are people around us right now, and I'm glad that I can witness this moment.

Kenny comes out and gives a ten minute warning, and everyone begins to clear out. When only Ben and I are left, I push away from him and circle him. Skating the entire length of the rink, I finally find my feet on the ice, and when I'm across the rink from him, Ben gets this look in his eyes. Almost like this hockey mode kicks in and he races up to me, waiting until the last second to cut the ice at a ninety-degree angle to stop, spraying my shins with shaved ice.

Shocked, all I can do is laugh. "Now I'm all wet."

He winks. "Now?"

I suck in a sharp breath, caught off guard and turned on even more than I was before.

Licking my lips, I push him playfully again and skate away, but he just races up beside me and stops in front of me.

I'm tall, but he still towers over me by a good six inches.

"You can't just run away from me."

"I wasn't running. I can't run in skates."

"Clever." He smirks, and the air between us crackles. Ben licks his lips, and the sight of it has me thinking about his tongue dragging across my skin.

Okay, I need a drink.

"I'm, uhm, starting to get cold. Do you think we could do the whiskey tasting now?"

"Sure," he grunts, and we skate off the ice to change back into our shoes.

We find Charlie sweeping around the distillery when we head inside, and Ben calls out to him, "Hey, you can go home early."

"You sure?"

"Yeah, Leah and I are just going to have a little tasting."

"You are, are you?" he says sarcastically, smiling.

"Shut up, man, get out of here." Charlie doesn't hide his wide grin as he grabs his keys and coat.

Alone now, I take a seat at the bar and watch as Ben pulls down various bottles from the shelves and lines up five glasses for each of us.

"Five?"

"I want to be thorough. I promised you a tasting."

Yes, he did, but he's also about to get me drunk. And I can't be held responsible for what I do or say when I am.

Ben pours two shots of each whiskey into every glass and then comes around to sit beside me.

"This first one is mellow. It's smooth and soft on the

pallet without having an intense alcohol reaction to your senses. It's a good one for beginners."

I love when he talks about his products. His passion slips through and it's incredibly sexy. Taking a sip, I do notice how it's softer on my palate than the one he gave me last week. "Which did I have at the gala?"

"This last one here." He taps the rim of the fifth glass. "It's not for beginners."

"But you had me try it anyway?"

"I wanted to see if you could handle it."

Smiling, I knock back the rest of the whiskey in my glass. "Did I pass your test?"

"You did. But with this next one," he says as smoothly as the whiskey coating my insides, "take your time to really let the flavors expand in your mouth before swallowing."

My head spins.

Is he still talking about whiskey?

I take a sip from the next glass he has lined up and do as he said, letting it sit on my tongue for a moment before swallowing.

"What did you taste this time?"

"It was a little more smokey?" I guess, unsure of anything right now.

"That's right." He scoots his chair a little closer when he reaches for his own glass. "Good job."

Ben's praise is like a shot to my core, making my clit throb, needing his attention and praise, too.

This is how it goes for the next three whiskeys, and I'm starting to feel it. My brain and body are both loose with their needs, and at some point, our legs became entangled. Each whiskey we tried had Ben inching closer to me. First just our thighs touched, then he turned so we faced each other, and then he proceeded to move closer with every reach for a glass he made until our legs were sandwiched together.

Ben places his hand on my knee and my pulse pounds in my ears. "Are there any others you want me to try?" I ask, breathless.

Every move he makes is a straight shot to my core, and with the whiskey already flowing through my veins, every brush of him against me is heightened. I could burst at any moment.

"No, that's it," he tells me, but there's a glint in his eyes that says otherwise.

His hair is messy from him running his hand through it, and I want nothing more than to do the same, just to see how it feels. Just as I want to run my fingertips over his beard and down his neck to feel his pulse thrumming beneath his skin. To feel his life.

He may think that living is hiding, but inside I know there's someone wanting more.

I take a deep breath to try and calm myself, but immediately regret it when his cologne fills my senses, making me dizzy with lust.

"Are there any ones here you have that you don't make yourself?"

"Yes, of course. But ours are better," he says, my eyes locked on his mouth.

"Yeah, yours is better." I lick my lips, then whisper, "I

think you gave me a little too much. I'm not going to be able to drive back to the inn."

"You were never driving back to the inn, Leah."

"What do you mean?"

He licks his lips and my eyes follow the movement with rapt attention, wanting to do the same with my tongue across his full lips.

Ben leans in closer, and with one arm resting on the bar, his hand flexes, the muscles in his forearm jumping like ropes being pulled tight.

"I planned on showing you exactly how addicted I want you. Step one, my pancakes. Step two, my whiskey."

He pauses, and I find the voice to ask, "What's step three?"

He leans in closer. I can see a smattering of freckles across his nose and cheeks, and his thick black eyelashes blink, giving way to the midnight blue of his eyes turning into a raging sea at night, daring me to jump in. Begging me to jump in and take the plunge – to let myself drown in the unknown depth.

Ben leans in even closer, his hand sliding up my leg, the span of it so big that it can almost cover the width of my thigh. His other hand comes up and cups the side of my neck, tilting my head back. My lips separate. My breath comes short. I know he can see the flushed look to my cheeks, and it's not just from the whiskey.

Sliding his nose down the bridge of my own, his lips hover above mine. "This is step three," he whispers, crushing his lips to mine.

It's not soft.

It's not sweet.

It's the outpouring of tension crashing down, like the waves of a tsunami unleashing their power after the sea has been drawn back to build. His hand grips my thigh, the other sliding to the back of my head to hold me exactly where he wants me.

Whiskey and fire set my veins ablaze and my hands go straight to his chest, gripping his shirt and pulling him closer. I want to claw my way inside of him. I want the fire to keep consuming me, to keep raging, but I don't know how I can take any more.

Ben's tongue sweeps across the seam of my lips and I moan into him, giving him access to me, and letting him take whatever he wants. I'm willing to give him that because I want to take everything right back from him.

He groans, and it's the sweetest sound I've ever heard.

He's devouring my mouth, and when I can't breathe anymore, I tear my lips away.

"Ben," I pant, trying to catch my breath.

He stands and spins me on my stool so my back is to the bar as he steps between my thighs, spreading them apart. I wrap my legs around his hips and he grips the bar's edge on either side of me.

"God, Leah, I've wanted to do that every day. Every fucking day."

"Me too," I admit, and the look in his eyes makes me feel like prey finally being caught. Sliding my hands up his torso and chest, I wrap them around the back of his neck and pull him down. "You wanted me addicted, and I am. I want more."

With a deep growl, his lips fuse to mine again and I tighten my legs around his hips while I practically claw my way up him.

"Ben, please," I manage to say, and he kisses his way across my jaw and down my neck, biting gently at the spot where my neck meets my shoulder.

"God, you smell amazing, you taste amazing, and fuck," he groans, "I need more, Leah. I need to taste more of you. I want all of you."

"Take whatever you want, Ben," I tell him, and his eyes flare.

Pushing the whiskey bottles and glasses to the side, he lifts me up onto the bar. His hands reach for my sweater, but I place mine over his, nervous. I know he wants me, but self-doubt creeps in knowing he's about to see me naked. I know he can see the brief moment of insecurity written on my face and he slides his hands out from under mine to rest them on top instead. He pulls them away from the hem of my sweater and places them at my sides.

"I want to see you, Leah. All of you. And trust me when I say, I fucking want you. I want every inch of you. I want to feel you. I want to memorize you. I want *everything*," he emphasizes. "I want it all."

I'm dizzy.

I can't even begin to process what he just said because my heart is racing, and all I manage to squeak out is a meager, "Okay."

He flashes me a grin that, if I wasn't already sitting, would make me fall to my knees

Ben lifts my sweater up and over my head, his eyes flashing with possession when they rake over my chest.

"Let me taste you, Leah."

Words won't even form anymore, and so I give him a small nod, his mouth already descending. He licks the mounds of my breasts above the cups of my bra, his hot tongue on my skin like nothing I've ever felt before.

His hands slide up my sides and I'm no longer self-conscience in the least. I've never felt more wanted or desired than I do in this moment. Unhooking my bra, Ben slides the straps down my arms and peels the fabric away from me.

"Jesus Christ," he breathes. "You're beautiful. Perfect."

Taking my nipple in his mouth, I cry out at the sudden onslaught of electricity bolting through me, and I have to grip the edge of the bar so I don't fall backwards.

Ben licks and sucks his way across both of my breasts, his large hands filled with my flesh, knowing exactly how to knead and squeeze them to make me squirm.

"Ben," I moan, begging, "please."

I know I'm drenched through my panties, my core throbbing and in need of his attention.

His hands slide back down my stomach, unbuttoning my jeans and pulling the zipper down. "Lift up, baby," he instructs, and I do as he says so he can peel my skin tight jeans down my legs. When he gets to my boots, he unzips them and they drop to the floor in a dull thud before my jeans follow suit. The only thing left covering me is my panties.

"No one's going to see us, right?" I ask, not even thinking about that before now, too lost in letting myself be worshipped by this man.

"There's no one here but us. The doors are locked and the windows are tinted. I wouldn't let anyone see you like this. You're for my eyes only."

Gripping my knees, he spreads my thighs, his eyes at their apex. "I've never seen a sexier sight," he whispers, kissing me from my knee to my hip, avoiding where I need him most. Ben repeats the same path on my other leg and I feel myself growing wetter and wetter, and I know he can see the evidence of that.

Sliding his nose along the seam of my panties, he takes a deep breath in, groaning. "I can smell how much you want me."

"Yes," I sigh, squirming in front of him. I need him to touch me. I need him to do *something* before I go crazy.

"I can see how much you want me, too. This thin lace separating me from heaven is clinging to your drenched pussy."

"Ben," I moan, begging shamelessly again, "please."

"Please, what?" His eyes find mine from between my thighs.

"Please, touch me," I whisper, and he smirks.

"I'm going to do so much more than just touch you, Leah," he promises, and his mouth descends on me, sucking on my lips through my panties.

I cry out, my hips lifting, pushing myself into his mouth

further.

His hot tongue presses down on my clit through the lace, and the slight roughness of the fabric combined with his heat has me biting my lip, trying not to scream out at how good it feels.

Ben finally pulls the lace to the side and groans, sliding his finger through my slick folds. "You're so wet." If my brain was working correctly, I'd think he sounded almost astonished at that fact, but I can't be certain when I barely have control over anything at the moment. Only the blind desire coursing through me. "This is all for me."

"Yes," I sigh.

"This has been waiting for me?"

"Yes," I admit, and he swirls his finger around my entrance, not going any further.

My vision blurs.

His broad shoulders are holding my legs open, and the moment his tongue touches me with nothing between us, I'm lost. I'm done. He swirls around my clit, putting pressure on it while his finger continues to swirl around my entrance.

I can't even feel myself anymore. I'm at Ben's mercy.

I'll never be the same after this. I already know that, and I've already accepted it.

I'm blinded by the greatest pleasure of my entire life.

Ben eats me like a starved man having a feast laid out before him. He inserts a single finger, then two, spreading them apart inside of me. White spots dot my vision and I don't know how much more I can take.

My sighs, moans, and pleas for more are just empty

words to my ears when all I can hear is my blood rushing, my heart racing, and the sound of Ben's groans with every swirl of his tongue.

The moment he curls his fingers inside of me, stroking my front wall while sucking my clit between his lips as hard as he can, I'm done. I'm gone. I'm lost.

I have no choice but to let go, falling back onto the bar.

My thighs squeeze his shoulders for dear life until I start to drift away. And when I come to again, it's to the gentle lapping of his tongue cleaning me and making sure he captures every last drop of his victory.

Ben didn't just give me an orgasm, he took it from me. And he can take as much as he wants from me if I get to experience that again.

Stepping back from between my thighs, his eyes lock with mine while he makes a show of gliding his tongue across his lips before bringing his glistening fingers to his mouth.

"What do I taste like?" I find myself asking boldly, my brain still recovering.

"Like heaven, Leah. Like sweet, sweet, heaven." Sitting on the stool between my legs, he licks his fingers clean and then grabs the closest bottle of whiskey, pouring himself a hefty portion in a glass. His eyes roam over my flushed and spent body as he sips his drink, not a single inch of me left untouched by his gaze.

The fog begins to clear from my brain and I come to realize how exposed I am like this before him. He has one hand resting on my thigh, his fingers gently stroking my flesh, and I blink, his handsome face coming into focus.

This is a fantasy.

How can this be real?

Ben takes another sip of whiskey and his tongue darts out to catch a stray drop left behind. I want to do that.

I will myself to find the strength to sit up, and I try and close my legs, but Ben's body prevents that. In fact, he scoots his stool closer to ensure the impossibility of that happening.

"I'm not anywhere near being done with you yet."

The rough edge of his voice has me ready for more and I reach out, running my hands through his hair, whispering, "Now who's addicted?"

His smirk holds everything as he takes another sip of whiskey. "I never said it'd be one-sided."

With him being so tall, we're practically at eye-level with the both of us sitting, and all I have to do is lean forward a few inches to kiss him.

The whiskey on his lips is the best tasting of them all from tonight, and if I wasn't already tipsy, I would most certainly be now.

"You're so beautiful, Leah," he murmurs against my lips, causing a warmth to spread from my chest, hearing the truth in his voice.

Now, I know I'm beautiful. I've never needed that validation from anyone. But it's different hearing it from someone in such an intimate setting and them saying it with such sincerity to make me not just know or believe it, but to *feel* it. Not just on the surface, but bone deep. In my soul, I can feel his words. It's not a lie and it's not a ploy to get my clothes off. We're already past that. He doesn't *have* to compliment me, and yet he does.

"Ben." My fingers brush across his cheek and jaw, and he leans into my touch, closing his eyes.

I'm scared. I want to be in the moment, but my mind is going through all the reasons why this shouldn't have happened, can't happen again, and can't go any further. But I don't care. Because no matter what happens, this feeling that he's given me is something I always want to hold onto. And since I'm already naked and on his bar, I might as well give in fully.

Taking my hand from his cheek, Ben kisses my palm and places it on the bar, leaning his forehead against mine.

"You know when I stayed with you, that morning when I woke up, all I could think about was you. I was frustrated, and I…" I trail off, wondering why I'm even sharing this with him now.

"And what?" he prompts, his hands sliding up and down my back.

"I touched myself," I whisper, "thinking about you and knowing you were somewhere in the house. I was pretending it was you there with me, but I knew if you really were, then it would be so much better than just my own fingers."

"Fucking Christ, Leah," he groans, pinching his eyes closed. His fingers dig into my lower back, pressing me closer to him. "Are you telling me you made yourself come in a bed in my house, thinking about me?" His voice is strained, almost like it pains him to know this.

"Yes," I confirm, and he huffs out a breath that blows across my lips.

"Fuck," he growls, slamming his mouth down on mine and pulling me flush against him, kissing the breath right out of me. "I can't wait to have all of you."

"Please, Ben," I whine. "I need you. All of you."

I run my hands under his shirt, his hard muscles contracting under my touch. The same muscles I saw on display when he was working out...and they're amazing. Each dip and mound is a testament to his hard work.

Ben only breaks our kiss long enough to tear his sweater off and then his lips are back on mine, eager and insistent.

I place my palms on his chest and I can feel his heart pounding. Sliding them up around his neck, I grip the hair at the nape of his neck, making him groan into me.

Ben pops his jeans open and shoves them down just far enough to free himself. He grips my hips and slides me forward to the edge of the bar. I can feel his hard length against my inner thigh and I bite back a moan, wanting him inside of me.

His grip tightens on my hips, his fingers digging into my soft flesh. "Shit, Leah. I don't have a condom. I didn't think... I didn't think I'd need one."

Panting, I scratch my nails across his shoulders. "I'm on the pill." I swallow hard, then confess softly, "I haven't done this in a long time."

His nose brushes across my cheek. "I've always used a condom."

"Me too. Ben, please."

"Are you sure?" He's giving me a chance to change my mind, but I don't want one. I don't need one.

"Yes," I sigh, and he captures my lips with his, sealing our fate.

There's no going back from this.

I've never let a man inside of me without protection because I never felt them worthy. It's an intimate thing. The most intimate. You're joined together with nothing separating you.

When I feel the tip of his cock at my entrance, I moan into our kiss, already knowing he's big by the fact that he has to stretch me open to push his broad head inside of me instead of just slipping right in with how wet I am. I know he's going to wreck me in the best possible way.

I squeeze around him inadvertently and he grunts, biting down on my bottom lip. "You're strangling me, Leah," he rasps, pushing forward.

I tense up, afraid he'll be too much for me, and his hands slide up and down my back.

Licking the shell of my ear, he whispers roughly, "Relax. I promise you'll be okay. I'm going to take care of you."

"I don't want you to be gentle though."

A primal sound of approval rumbles out of him and Ben's fingers dig into the soft flesh of my hips as he thrusts into me fully. My neck falls back and I cry out, my body feeling like it's being split in two. He stills inside of me, allowing me to adjust to his size.

I don't even understand how he fits, but it's the most glorious of feelings to have him stretching me and filling me to the point of pain. Stuffed, is the only word that comes to mind since I'm currently losing mine.

"You still don't want me to be gentle?" he rasps in my ear.

Moaning, I lull my head to the side, gripping his biceps. "No. Don't be gentle." Ben brings my face back up to look into my eyes, and I add, "I want you to give me you."

A look of pure determination crosses his face and he pulls out, stilling for a moment, and then slams back inside of me. I cry out again. Spread out on the bar like this, he hits a spot inside of me so deep, it's like he's trying to unknot my stomach.

Ben pulls out a few inches and slams back in, then pulls out even more and slams back in. He finds a rhythm, and I don't even know who I am or where I am. The world around me blurs while the greatest pleasure I've ever known floods my body, taking over it entirely.

I'm drowning. I'm floating. I'm flying. I'm dragged down, and then pulled back up.

My arms give out and I fall back onto the bar.

Panting, I grip my breasts and roll my taut nipples between my fingers, crying out, feeling it as a straight shot to my core.

Ben's grunting is feral, and the way his muscles contract with every thrust has me mesmerized.

"I could fuck you all night," he growls out like an untamed beast, with wild and unruly hair to match. "It's too good, Leah. You're too good. I don't want it to end."

"Ben," I plea. "I can't hold on much longer."

"If I let you come, you have to promise me you'll let me fuck you all night."

"Yes!" I'm willing to agree to anything at this point. Especially if it's a demand for more. "I'll do anything!"

Victory flashes in his eyes and he presses his thumb down on my clit.

Screaming, I scratch at the top of the smooth bar, needing something, anything, to hold on to, but I come up empty. Wave after wave washes over me, pummeling me to where my bones and muscles feel as fluid as water.

My vison blurs and the only thing that penetrates this feeling of being under water is Ben's roar as he stills inside of me, filling me with his hot come.

Ben slides his hands to my back and pulls me up, wrapping his arms around me. We're both slick with a thin layer of sweat, and his lips meet mine with a hard kiss.

Leaning his forehead against mine, our ragged breaths mix, passing air to the other in an attempt to somehow catch our own.

"I'm going to hold you to your promise," he murmurs, and my lips turn up in a small grin.

"I never break my promises."

Ben gives me a soft kiss and pulls out. I feel the loss immediately. He fit too perfectly to not have him inside of me permanently, even though I know that's not possible.

I'm addicted and feeling crazy, and I'm scared of what that'll do to me.

Chapter 10

I look at myself in the mirror and try and tame my hair, but it's no use. My cheeks are flushed, my eyes are bright, and my lips are red and swollen from Ben's rough kisses.

It was the best sex of my life. Not that I've had an exorbitant amount or anything, but enough to know that I've been severely missing out.

Shaking my head, I take my time fixing my clothes and freshening up. When I emerge, I lean against the wall while Ben finishes cleaning up the bar. I definitely won't be able to look at it the same way again.

Biting my lip, I run my hands through my hair again. I can't believe I did that. I can't believe I just had sex with Ben at work, on his bar, with zero shame.

Washing his hands, Ben looks around and makes sure everything is in its place so no one will be the wiser tomorrow as to what we did in here.

He smiles when he spots me. "Ready to go?" he asks, and my stomach flips, wanting him all over again.

I give him a small nod and he takes four long strides to get to me, not stopping until my back is pressed against the wall and his hands are framing my face.

"I hate that you had to get dressed," he murmurs. "But now I get to undress you all over again in ten minutes."

"Ten minutes?" I question teasingly. "Are you sure we'll make it to your house in time?"

The same look of determination crosses his face as it did earlier. "If I don't, then I'll pull my truck over and take you right there on the side of the road." He leans in closer. "But I'd much rather have you in my bed so I can spread you out any way I please."

"Then you better hurry."

On a growl, Ben kisses me hard and quick before grabbing my hand and pulling me through The Whiskey Room's exit, only pausing to lock the door again. He keeps pulling me along to his truck, and when he opens the passenger side door, he practically tosses me up inside, my skin heating at how strong he is.

I can't help but laugh when he tears out of the parking lot and down the empty road to his house, loving how eager he is.

We pull into his garage and he presses the button so the door closes behind us. "I think that was less than ten," I tell him, and he hops out, coming around to my side to pull me out and press me against the side of his truck.

"I take my challenges seriously," he says, his mouth on mine in an instant. This kiss isn't rushed. It's long and languid, and my body melts against his truck, needing it to hold me up. His tongue sweeps through my mouth, and while I moan, he groans, pulling back.

"I need to get you upstairs. I want to lay you out on my bed so I can fuck you right."

My head spins at his dirty words as he pulls me through his house, up the stairs, and down the hall to his bedroom. I don't even know how my legs were able to work, but the next thing I know, my back is hitting his mattress and his hands are all over me, taking my clothes off for the second time tonight.

I'm splayed before him in only my panties like on the bar, when he says, "Now, this is a sight I could get used to. So fucking beautiful." He rubs his jaw, taking me in from head to toe. "I already know what's waiting for me beneath that little scrap of lace and I can't wait another second." Gripping the waistband of my panties in his hands, he slides them down my legs, leaving me completely naked while he remains fully dressed, towering over me at the foot of the bed.

There's no room for self-consciousness, because with the heat in his eyes, there's no way I could feel anything less than beautiful and desired.

"You said you thought of me that morning you woke up here." I nod my head. "Show me what you did."

"What?" I squeak out.

"Show me what you did," he repeats, his voice dropping an octave, leaving no room for argument. Ben pulls the chair that's in the corner of the room to the end of the bed and takes a seat, lifting his leg to rest his ankle on his opposite knee. "Don't get shy on my now. I want to see you touch yourself, Leah."

Closing my eyes, I bend my knees and slide my feet up towards me, running my hands down my thighs and spreading my knees apart.

Ben groans. "Eyes open and on me, Leah."

I peel mine open to find his zeroed in on the spot between my legs. He licks his lips and rubs his jaw, his other hand flexing on the arm of his chair.

"I've never done this before," I whisper. No man has ever asked me to. I'm nervous, but I can't deny him with the way he's looking at me.

Gliding my tongue across my bottom lip, I take it between my teeth and slide a single finger through my wet folds. The cool air hitting my exposed, wet flesh sends a shiver through me.

I dip two fingers inside of me and bring them up to my clit, rubbing circles around the tight bundle of nerves, over and over again. My legs start to shake, and while my eyes fall closed once more, I use everything in me to open them again, clashing with Ben's deep blue ones straight away. He's watching me with an intensity that makes my skin break out in goosebumps.

Unbuttoning his pants, Ben reaches inside and frees

himself from the tight confines. Gently stroking his length from base to tip, my mouth waters at the sight, and I feel myself grow wetter. I didn't get to see him before in the heat of the moment, but his cock is long and thick, with bulging veins and a swollen, mushroomed head I want to feel stretching me open again.

The sight of him stroking himself is what I need to push me over the edge, picturing him inside of me. The memory is still so fresh. I press down hard on my clit and let go.

Ben lets out a deep groan. "Fuck, Leah."

I hear the faint sounds of his clothes hitting the floor and then the bed dips, his body covering mine.

"That was the sexiest fucking thing I've ever seen," he rasps, licking the column of my neck. His teeth graze my jawline before he bites my chin and then kisses me long and slow, savoring me. "The sexiest fucking thing, Leah," he murmurs against my lips, then kisses me harder.

I feel him at my entrance, and he swallows my moan as he enters me in a single thrust, spearing me with his cock.

My back arches off the bed and I grip the sheets on either side of me.

Ben pounds into me hard and fast, unable to hold back. And just when I feel myself reaching the edge again, he pulls out of me.

"No!" I cry out.

Flipping me over onto my stomach, he lifts my hips so my ass is in the air and spreads my knees apart, sliding right back into me. My grunts and moans are muffled by the pillows as he goes back to pounding into me.

Ben's fingers dig into my sides and he slaps my ass. He's going even deeper at this angle, and every hit home has me groaning.

I'm at his mercy.

I press my hands flat against the headboard and take what he gives me, loving what he gives me.

He slaps my ass again and I squeeze around him, making him grunt. The vibrations travel through me and it's like sound waves – ripples of energy reaching every corner of my body.

"Come for me, Leah," Ben commands, slapping my ass again.

I cry out, biting the pillow in front me as my body convulses around him, squeezing him. He pumps into me a few more times before pulling out and groaning, a warmth hitting my back and dripping down my sides.

He just came on my back and I've never felt sexier.

Falling to the bed, Ben collapses next to me and pulls me on top of him so I'm half draped across his chest.

"You just came all over me," I whisper.

"I did. And you're going to leave it there until I'm done with you."

"Okay," I say sleepily, my eyes already closed, loving the possessiveness to his demand.

❄ ❄ ❄ ❄

The gentle swirl of fingers on my skin wakes me from a deep sleep – up and down my back and then around to my chest. Ben creates random patters on my breasts, hips, stomach, and then back up to swirl around my nipples, never touching them.

His hot mouth then follows the same pathway as his fingertips and I sigh, my eyes still closed, just savoring the feeling of being worshipped like this. It's tender and intimate.

When he finally gives in and swirls his tongue around my peaked nipples, I arch into him, holding his head to my breast. Moaning his name, my hips rock, trying to find some sort of relief with our legs entwined.

He licks, sucks, and bites his way around both of my breasts, making me grow wetter and wetter to the point where I know I'm dripping on him, but he still just takes his time enjoying himself.

"Your tits are perfect," he murmurs against my skin, continuing to torture me with his slow appreciation.

He's in no rush for more, but I am.

I'm panting his name, begging him for more, and he grazes the tip of my nipple with his teeth, making me cry out.

Ben rolls onto his back and takes me with him so I'm straddling his hips. "I want you to ride me, baby."

Looking down at him from this angle, it's almost hard to believe that this is real with him. But there's no mistaking or faking this. His hands cup my breasts and he licks his lips as if he misses the taste of them.

"I want you to ride me. I want to see these bouncing and swaying right above my face. I want to watch you while you take what you need and I enjoy the show."

His words only make me blinder with lust.

His thick cock is so heavy, that even when hard as a steel pipe, it lays flat against his stomach.

Ben grips my hips and helps me slide up his length, his eyes pinching closed for a second as I rock my hips. That look on his face… I wish I could take a picture so I'll always have it to remember how I can make this man feel.

His hands move around to grip my ass, his fingertips digging into my ample flesh.

Reaching down, I position him at my entrance and brace myself on his chest. I sink down on him until he's fully seated inside of me, and my head falls back, my mouth hanging open as a deep moan is torn from the depths of me.

It's different like this. It's different on top.

He hits a different spot, a deeper spot, and I can't move yet.

One of Ben's hands leaves my ass, and the next thing I know, a quick sting flashes across my skin where he was gripping me and I feel the vibrations of his slap travel through me from where we're connected.

I squeeze him inside of me and he grunts.

"Do it again," he demands, his voice holding a ring of authority to it that makes me want to do exactly as he says. He slaps my other ass cheek and I squeeze him inside of me again, making him groan.

My fingers curl into him, my nails biting the flesh of his chest. The possessive part of me wishes I could leave a permanent mark on him so that any woman after me will know that I was here. And another, even more possessive part of me, doesn't want there to be another woman after me.

"I need you to move, Leah."

Looking down at him, I smirk. "I thought you wanted me take what I want. And I am." Squeezing around him again, he grunts, his hands moving from my ass to my breasts, squeezing them and pinching my nipples.

I cry out and he smirks. "I'm taking what I want, too."

Digging my nails into his chest even more, I start to rock my hips, straight shots of lightning bursting from where we're joined.

I close my eyes, letting myself get lost in the moment – in him.

I slide myself up and down his length, my muscles clamping down on him with every drag up, and spreading wide with every drop down.

My pace becomes too quick and erratic, and I'm so lost and blind in taking what I want that I don't even have the brain capacity to care what I look like right now. I don't care if my stomach is jiggling or if I'm too heavy to be on top of him. I don't care. I take what I need.

Ben must know how lost I am, because he takes control by grabbing my ass, pulling my cheeks apart with his tight grip and guiding me to a rhythm that has my orgasm building in seconds.

Helping me ride him, he sets the pace. Slow, then quick. Slow, then quick. His hips roll up into mine with every thrust, rubbing my clit in just the right way.

My moans echo in my head and I peel my eyes open to look down at him, his face blurry and hazy through the lenses of my lust. I know his face mirrors mine, though, and it's all I need. The next roll of his hips has my inner muscles fluttering, and then I'm pushed off the edge so I'm falling into the empty abyss, not knowing where I'll land.

My nails rake down his chest and my neck arches backwards, a long and low moan pulled from me while I pulse around him. And before the waves even have a chance to subside, Ben flips our positions and presses my knees to my chest, pumping through my orgasm.

"You looked so fucking beautiful taking what you needed from me." Ben continues to piston me and I feel another orgasm building, already knowing it's going to be bigger than the last.

His hands grip my shins, not letting me move while *he* takes from *me* this time. There's something so erotic and sexy about him putting me where he wants me and taking and doing what he wants, but still giving me everything in return.

I claw at the sheets, my breasts bouncing and swaying with every hard thrust.

Ben grunts, looking down at me. "I can't stop fucking you. It's too good."

"Ben," I moan, chanting incoherent thoughts, then beg, "please."

Groaning, he pushes my legs up and apart even more. "Open your eyes," he demands, and when I manage to meet his above me, his dark blue ones are swirling with untamed desire. For me. Because of me. His hair is damp from sweat, hanging around his face, and his jaw clenches. "Come for me, Leah. Now."

"Not until you," I manage to get out, and he growls,

dropping lower to the bed and lifting my hips so he hits me at a greater angle. We both groan.

"Fuck," he grunts, and it only takes three more thrusts for me to see stars dancing in front of my eyes.

He releases my legs and presses down on my clit, the stars now bursting like fireworks in my vision. My eyes start to roll back, and the last thing I register is Ben's face above me, so beautiful as he finds his pleasure inside of me. Then it's just darkness.

I don't fight the pull under, instead going with the urge to let myself drown in the sea of Ben.

Chapter 11

I can't believe he made come so hard I saw stars and practically passed out. That's never happened before. I didn't even know it was possible, but Ben has me so hyper-tuned to every touch and every feeling that I was on overdrive and had no choice but to give in.

The morning light is streaming in through the windows and I wiggle my way out from under his arm to pad across his room to the bathroom. Quickly using it, I splash some cool water on my face and study myself in the mirror. My breasts have marks from his mouth and my hips have marks from his fingers, but it's the marks I can't see that have me blushing. The marks inside my body from where he's been, including my heart.

I look over my shoulder in the mirror and see Ben standing in the doorway, his eyes roaming over my naked body. And even in the harsh light of the bathroom, he still looks at me like I'm the most beautiful woman in the world.

Coming up behind me, he grips the edge of the counter on either side of me, his body molding to mine. I can feel his hard length growing against my back and I bite my lip, pressing back into him.

He wraps one of his arms across my stomach like a bar and holds me to him, nuzzling my neck and whispering in my ear, "How about we take a shower?"

Stepping away from me, Ben starts the water, and when the steam fogs the glass, he takes my hand and pulls me in with him. Pressing me against the cold tiles, he tilts my chin up and I look into his dark blue eyes, smiling.

"What's that look for?" he asks, water dripping from the tips of his hair onto my face.

"Nothing. I'm just...happy."

A smile grows across his face until he's blinding me with his perfect teeth. I've never seen him look like this, and he's beautiful. So handsome.

"It's been a while, but I think I am too."

I raise my eyebrows, skirting my fingers up and down the sides of his torso. "You think?"

"No, I know I am," he says, and his simple admission makes my heart clench, both in sadness because he hasn't been happy, and in elation that it's me he's feeling happy with.

Leaning up on my toes, I press my lips to his and slide

my hands up his chest and through his wet hair. Gliding my tongue across his bottom lip, I kiss him slow, wanting to memorize his taste. And because of that, I have the urge to do something I haven't in a long time. Lowering myself back onto my feet, I look up at him mischievously, chewing my bottom lip.

"What's that look for?" he asks right before I slide down the tiles to my knees before him. His eyes turn thunderously dark and his arms flex as he presses his palms to the tiles above me.

I take him in my hand and it doesn't even fit all the way around. I don't know how he's going to fit in my mouth, but I'm going to try. I want to know what this man tastes like.

I run my nails up and down his length, gently scratching his sensitive flesh, making him shudder. He's heavy and warm, and I can feel his eyes on me – empowering me and giving me a burst of courage.

With the swollen mushroomed head of his cock just an inch from my lips, I look up at him. "I don't know if you'll fit in my mouth."

His jaw flexes, his one hand coming down to brush his fingers across my cheek. "You're going to take as much of me as you can."

It's a statement, a command, a challenge, and I find myself saying softly, "Okay."

With determination, I suck the head of his cock into my mouth, and Ben groans. My eyes flash up to his as I swirl my tongue around him before taking as much of him as I can. I relax my jaw, but I can't even get half of him in my mouth.

Not even close.

When he's as deep as I can take him without gagging, I pull back and swirl my tongue around his head.

Fisting the base of his cock, I work the part of him I can't fit in my mouth and find my rhythm. Ben grunts, his arms falling forward so his forearms are resting on the tiles.

I can feel him grow inside my mouth and I reach around to grip his firm, round ass, holding him to me as I take as much of him as I can, swallowing around him.

Ben groans and my eyes flash up to his, his forehead resting against the tiles, his dark eyes glued to mine.

"Again," he commands, and I swallow around him again.

I bob back up his length and then take him deep once more. And when I swallow this time, he lets out a long and low groan that I can feel travel through me as hot spurts of come shoot down my throat. I keep swallowing until I've taken every last drop I've earned and then release him with a wet pop.

Ben grips me beneath my arms and lifts me to my feet, pressing me against the tiles and capturing my lips with his. "I thought you splayed out on my bed last night was the sexiest thing I've ever seen, but I was wrong. You on your knees before me, taking me in your hot little mouth, is the sexiest thing I've ever seen." Nipping my bottom lip, he sucks it between his, then smooths it out with his tongue. "Now let me take care of you," he whispers against my lips.

Reaching for the soap, he lathers his hands and runs them all over my body, cleaning me. He doesn't let me do a thing besides stand here and allow him to care for me. He's gentle and doesn't try for anything more. I don't even know if I can take any more after last night and this morning, but because he's not trying for more, I need him even more.

Ben squats to run his hands down each of my legs, and when he stands back up, he goes to run his hand over my hip, but I grab it first. His brows come together in confusion until I guide his hand between my legs, widening my stance as an invitation.

I don't even need to say anything. He already knows.

Slipping his fingers right inside of me, it doesn't take long before I'm fluttering around him and he wraps his arm around me to keep me upright while he presses his lips to mine and swallows my moan, taking it for himself.

When my orgasm subsides, Ben removes his fingers and goes back to washing me like nothing happened. Next is my hair, and he shampoos and conditions it, making sure to massage my scalp as he does.

I'm so relaxed by the end of the shower, all I can do is lean against the wall and watch as Ben washes himself.

My God, he's a work of art.

When he's finished, he turns the water off and reaches for the towels, patting me dry and wrapping one around me before doing the same for himself.

I look at my jeans and sweater on the floor of his room, not really wanting to put them back on. I don't have to worry about it though, because Ben hands me a pair of sweatpants and a t-shirt with a smirk. "I liked the way you looked in my clothes."

"And I liked wearing them." I put my bra on and slip

into the soft fabrics of his clothes, using the towel to get the excess water out of my hair. I don't put my panties back on though, and when I look back at Ben, his eyes darken, knowing I'm not wearing any. "Problem?"

"Not at all," he rasps, kissing me hard and quick. "I'm going to make us breakfast."

"Okay," I sigh. "I will have to go back to the inn to change before work, though.

"Not a problem."

Picking up my jeans and sweater, I fold them neatly and carry them downstairs. Ben makes me coffee and then gets to work on pancakes and scrambled eggs, and I'm in heaven.

Mind blowing sex with Ben, waking up in his arms, and now he's cooking me breakfast... He's the whole package.

After eating, Ben drives me back to the inn. "I'll wait for you."

"You don't have to do that."

"I want to. And besides, how else would you get to work?" he asks, and my eyes scan the parking lot. Oh, right, my car is still at the winery.

"I might be longer than five minutes, though."

"It's okay. Take your time."

I smile. "Alright."

Hopping out of his truck, I keep my folded clothes stuffed inside my jacket as I hurry inside, giving a small wave to the lady behind the front desk.

I get ready as quickly as I can, putting on an outfit that reflects how I'm feeling. After last night, that would be sexy and bold. I put on tights, over-the-knee leather heeled boots, and a plum sweater dress that hugs me in all the right places, hitting my legs mid-thigh. I add a long necklace, earrings, my watch, and then get to work on finishing drying my hair and applying my makeup.

I feel like I look different, even though I don't. At least, not drastically. It's probably the countless orgasms I had last night and this morning that's making me glow.

Grabbing my work bag and my purse, I hurry back out to Ben and feel his eyes on me the entire walk across the parking lot. My coat is the same length as my dress, so all he sees are my tights and boots, and when I'm back in the warmth of his truck, his hand comes to rest on my thigh.

"You better be wearing something under here."

"What kind of girl do you take me for?" I tease. "Of course I am." I unbutton my jacket to show him my dress beneath, and Ben's teeth scrape his bottom lip.

"You expect me to work today knowing you're wearing this?"

"I dress like this every day, and you've managed to work just fine thus far."

"No, I haven't."

Smiling, I cover his hand on my leg with my own. "Well, I would say I'm sorry, but I'm not."

With a small smile, he shakes his head, pulling out of the inn's lot and heading for Breaker Estates.

When we walk in, Charlie is taking bottles of whiskey from a wooden crate and placing them on the shelf behind the bar in the tasting room.

Spotting us coming in together, he grins like a fool. "Car

trouble, Leah? I saw yours was here when I came in."

"Oh, uhm, yes," I say, not believable in the least. "Ben just, uh, offered to drive me back after the tasting last night since I had a little too much." I'm babbling like an idiot and Ben doesn't even try to hide his grin.

He leans down to whisper in my ear, "A little too much of my dick in your tight pussy."

Sweet baby Jesus, my face turns beet red and my eyes widen. The audacity of this man to make me so flustered when I still have an entire day of work ahead of me.

"Alright!" I say a little too loudly, pressing my palms to my cheeks. "I'm going to get a cup of coffee."

"Don't hurry off on my account, Leah," Charlie says with a smile. "It's just good to know Ben can still be nice when he wants to be."

"I can also fire you whenever I want, too," Ben tells him, but Charlie just laughs him off.

"Then who would make you your award-winning whiskey, my friend?"

Ben grins and raises his hands in defeat. "Good point. Now," he says to me, "let's get you a coffee."

※ ※ ※ ※

The morning goes by smoothly and it's mid-afternoon when Ben comes down to see me.

"Hey."

"Hi." I smile.

"I'm here to make sure you eat lunch today."

"Oh," I say, surprised, then turn to Cindy, Ben's restaurant manager who's working the table with me. "You can handle things for a half hour, right?"

"Of course. Go eat and take a break."

I give her a warm smile and stand. "Thanks."

Ben places his hand on my lower back as we walk through the tasting room packed with people, and then a back way around the distillery that takes us to his office's staircase without being seen by anyone else.

"I already ordered us lunch. I hope you don't mind."

Looking at the plates of food on his desk, I smile. "I don't mind. Thank you." I sit on the chair in front of his desk and take a bite of the turkey club sandwich. "Ohmygod," I say in a rush. "This is good. I was starving."

"Glad to be of service."

Swallowing, I look up at him while he takes the seat across from me and give him a look. "You've been of great service to me."

Grunting, Ben rubs his jaw. "Leah."

"Yes?" I ask innocently, batting my lashes as I bite into a potato chip.

His eyes are smoldering now. "Don't act innocent when I know you're far from it."

"I don't know what you're talking about."

"I can remind you," he says gruffly, and my pulse skyrockets just thinking about him taking me up against the wall or on top of his desk

"I don't need reminding. Just eat your lunch."

"What if I said I was hungry for you?"

"I'd have to say too bad because we're both at work and I don't want to go back down there looking like I was just ravished by the man everyone saw me walk away with."

He flashes me a sexy little grin. "Ravished, huh?"

"Shut up and eat your sandwich."

He actually listens to me this time and we enjoy our lunch together. I give him a quick kiss afterwards and then saunter back downstairs.

I take a quick detour to the kitchen for coffee and manage to give Chef Casey a wave between him barking out orders. I'm pouring myself a cup of when Charlie comes in for the same fix.

"Hey, Leah. Will I see you tonight?"

My eyebrows come together. "Tonight?"

"Yeah, the cocktail competition is tonight. I'm packing up the crates of everything I'll need now."

"Wait, what do you mean you're packing up what you'll need? I didn't know Breaker Estates was competing. It wasn't in Janet's notes." Panic starts to set in and Charlie can sense that.

"Oh, I forgot to tell you." He at least has the decency to look sorry. "The coordinator of the festival reached out to ask if we wanted to fill a last-minute spot after a winery had to pull out. I've got it all covered though, so I don't want you to worry."

"You've got it covered?"

"Yes. They supply the booth, and all the people attending will have their own glasses for the drink samples as they walk around. So, all I need are the ingredients for our drink."

"What are you making?"

"My own creation," he says proudly. "I'm not clever with names, so I went with what it is – a whiskey and icewine. All cocktails have to be run by the coordinator to ensure no one is making the same thing, and each drink has to have icewine as an ingredient."

"So, it's just whiskey and icewine?"

"No. It's icewine, whiskey, and cabernet. I'm going to have a glass beverage dispenser of the mixture and then I'll top off each drink with seltzer and a strawberry slice once poured."

"Oh, that sounds really good."

"Come tonight and you can try it."

"Maybe I will. Do you have a sign for the drink so people know what's in it without you having to say it a thousand times? With the handles to all your social medias and website?"

"Oh, no, I don't. And we don't really have any social media accounts…"

Sighing, I roll my eyes. Of course they don't. God forbid Ben okays an Instagram account or Facebook page.

"Ben needs to step out of the dark ages and realize people love to tag where they are and look places up before they go to see if there are any cute places to stage pictures." I see Charlie's face go blank. He clearly doesn't know what I'm talking about.

"Could you do that for us?"

"I'm only here for the festival. Who would run it when

I'm gone?" That thought pangs my chest, so I change the subject to safer waters. "Do you also need a sign with the winery's name?"

"I have a tablecloth with our logo on it that will be draped over the booth."

"Good. Then I'll make a drink sign and frame it for you."

"I'm really sorry, Leah. I thought I had everything, under control. I should've told you."

"Yes, you should've." I tell him with some sass, flashing him a smile and taking my coffee back out to the tasting room.

❄ ❄ ❄ ❄

"How come you didn't tell me about the cocktail competition tonight?" I ask Ben, placing my hand on my hip.

"What about it?"

"That you're participating?" I say obviously.

"Charlie promised me he had it all under control and wouldn't need you for anything."

"He did need me for something, but I've handled it. And I want to go tonight. I was told it was the only way to try the drink Charlie's making. I don't want to go by myself, though." Biting my lip, I look at him expectantly, hoping he'll give in.

"With the way you're looking at me, I don't know how I can say no."

"Then you shouldn't. I can make it worth your while. I'll

even throw in dinner."

Ben leans forward and rests his forearms on his desk. "Make it worth my while how?"

"I think you know how," I say, doing my best to sound seductive. And it works, because Ben's jaw flexes.

"Deal."

"You don't even know the specifics."

"Oh, I know the specifics. You'll find out what I have in mind when it's time."

"Alright, then," I say breathless, my core clenching in anticipation.

An hour later, we go to dinner at a pub in town, and afterwards, I ask Ben to stop off at the inn so I can change into something warmer. I exchange my dress and tights for fleece lined leggings, a thick sweater, and my snow boots.

When we make it to Main Street where they have a portion of it blocked off, the gentle snow that started before dinner has now turned into a steady fall.

"I love that it's snowing," I say, looking up at him.

"You do?"

"Of course! Snow makes this whole thing seem so much more wintery and fun."

Wrapping his arm around me, he tucks me against his side as we walk up to the booth where you purchase your sampling glass and tokens for the cocktails from. The people working the booth recognize Ben right away and give us both a glass and a handful of tokens, saying all owners and participants are free. I even get a scorecard and pencil to rate each drink, and a ballot to fill out at the end for my top three cocktails.

Ben and I make our way around each of the booths, sampling the different cocktails. Each one is different and unique. Some have created decadent dessert cocktails using amaretto or kalua, while others use gin, whiskey, wine, or vodka.

I love the gin, icewine, and cranberry spritzer with a sprig of rosemary from one winery, and it's currently in my top spot, but I haven't gotten to try Charlie's yet. We finally make it over to his booth and I'm already working up a good buzz, so I give him a bright smile.

"Charlie!" I say a little too loudly. "I'm ready for you! Hit me with it!" I place my glass down with more vigor than necessary and he bellows out a deep laugh.

"I see you've made the rounds?"

"Yes, and I saved the best for last, my friend."

"That you did," he says proudly. "You two look like you're having fun."

"Yes, we are. Who knew all it took for this bear to loosen up was some liquor?" Laughing, Charlie pours us our drinks and Ben shakes his head. "Ohh, lovely presentation," I praise, admiring the fresh strawberry slice on the rim of my glass before taking a sip. "And we have a winner!" I exclaim, and the people beside us laugh.

"I think you're a little biased," Ben murmurs in my ear, and I turn to him, our faces close.

"I don't think so," I whisper, my cold breath blowing right against his lips.

Clearing my throat, I lean into him and sip my drink,

spotting Charlie's coy grin and the look that passes between him and Ben.

"I think I can accurately fill this out now," I state, pulling out my ballot and writing in Breaker Estates as number one, Pedler as number two, and Innis as number three. "Be right back," I tell them, and walk over to the ballot box on the judge's table a few booths down.

I make sure to get a refill of Charlie's cocktail and then proceed to drag Ben back around to the other ones that were favorites of mine so I can sample them all again. He remains by my side, and every time I look up at him to say something, I already find him looking at me. He keeps his hand on my lower back or his arm wrapped around me while we weave our way through the people, and it feels like we're a real couple. It feels so natural to be out with him like this.

"Are you having fun?" He has to lean down close to my ear in order for me to hear him over the live band, and I lean back into him, smiling.

"I am. Thank you for taking me."

"Like I said, I couldn't deny you." He kisses the spot below my ear and I sigh, closing my eyes at the feel of his cool lips against me.

This man...

How has he turned into this sweet and sexy man from the jerk I met a week and a half ago? And how am I supposed to go back to Toronto in just over a week and not still want him?

I don't want to think about that right now, though. I just want to enjoy this moment with him, and I know one surefire way to avoid thinking about what's next.

The band playing has the vibes and sound of an Irish pub rock band and I grab Ben's hand. "Dance with me."

"What?"

"Dance with me, Ben."

He's about to answer me when someone takes the microphone to announce that the panel of judges will be having their tasting now while the votes from the people in attendance are being tallied.

"Ah, saved just in time," he tells me, but I refuse to take that as an answer.

"Nope. You're going to dance with me after they announce the winners."

"We'll see."

"Yes, you will," I sass, pulling him along so we have a good view of the judges as they go through each winery's cocktails.

Waiting for them to deliberate has me bouncing from foot to foot. "Calm down," Ben insists, pulling my back to his front.

"I can't. I'm excited to see if you win."

"It would be Charlie winning, not me."

"The fact that you think that is so humbling and cute."

"Cute?" He chokes on the word, as if it's an affront to his manhood.

Sighing, I peer up at him. "Fine. Not cute. Incredibly sexy."

The smile he flashes me makes my heart ricochet in my chest, because he is indeed, incredibly sexy.

"And third place goes to…" the announcer drags out, gaining my attention again, "Innis!" The crowd cheers. "Second place goes to…Jackson Estates!" More cheers. "And the winner is…" Ben's arm tightens around me. "BREAKER ESTATES!" he yells into the microphone, and I scream.

"Ben! You won! I told you, you were the best! I knew it!" I look up at him and he spins me so I'm facing him, his face filled with pride and amazement.

I'm vaguely aware of the people around us staring, but quickly put them out of my mind when Ben does something I don't expect him to do. He pulls me against him and crushes his lips to mine. I press up on my toes and wrap my arms around his neck, my back bending with the intensity.

I give in fully, his cold lips setting mine on fire.

When I pull back, I'm breathless and panting for air in my constricted lungs. My head is spinning with the liquor and pure joy of being here for Ben when his winery gets the recognition it deserves. He's won plenty of awards for his whiskey and wine, but knowing him this short while, I doubt he's ever present for the praise.

I smile up at him. "That was unexpected."

"I couldn't resist."

Biting my lip, I scratch my fingers back and forth against the nape of his neck.

"Will you dance with me now?" The snow is falling heavier around us, making me feel like we're in our own little world, and before he has the chance to deny me, I grab his hand and pull him over to the area in front of the stage.

After only two songs though, Ben drags me over to the

side of the stage where we're hidden in the shadows to kiss me breathless again.

"Can I take you home yet?" he murmurs in my ear, nuzzling my neck. "I want to spend the entire night seeing how many times and how many different ways I can make you come before passing out again."

If I ever find myself saying no to an offer like that, I'm clearly on the brink of death.

And little does he know, I'm on the brink of passing out right now just hearing him say that.

"Yes," I sigh, and Ben doesn't waste any time. He takes my hand and leads me around the blockades to avoid all the people, making me laugh at his eagerness. How did I get so lucky?

"You're okay to drive, right?" I ask when we're safely in the cab of his truck.

"Those were little samples, Leah. I'm a big man."

I bite my lip, my eyes raking over him. "Yes, you are." I didn't really mean to say that out loud, but there's no taking it back, and Ben huffs out a laugh that has my insides melting.

"I also stopped before you. You just didn't notice."

Ben drives slow with the snow falling steadily, and when we get to his house, he fulfills his promise.

He first takes me bent over the back of his couch with half our clothes still on because he couldn't wait. Then he has me ride him on the couch after we catch our breath. We finally end up in his bed after he carries me upstairs so he can press my face into the pillows while he takes me from behind and slaps my ass until I scream.

I still don't pass out, though, my body knowing it can still take a little more.

It's not until he takes me slow, my orgasm building in me like the pull back of a bow and arrow, testing my tension strength until I snap and let go, flying high and seeing stars.

Ben Breaker just made an indelible mark on me.

There's no going back.

There's no recovering.

There's no possible way for me to be the same after him. I don't know if that's his intention, but it's what has happened. And if he didn't mean for it to be like this, then I know there's only one ending for us — me being left with my heart in pieces.

Chapter 12

"So, I was thinking we should get out of here for a little bit," Ben says to me in the kitchen while I'm pouring myself my afternoon cup of coffee.

"What do you mean, get out of here? It's the middle of the day and…" I tap my chin. "Oh, yeah, we're in the middle of a busy Saturday that's not supposed to end for another five hours."

He runs his hand down my arm. "Come on," he urges. "Everyone here has it covered. I want to take you into town so you can experience the pairings of some of the wineries."

I perk up. "Really? Well, then I'm sure Cindy can hold down the fort for a little while. I'm in."

Giving me one of his rare smiles, he plants a quick kiss

on my cheek. "I'll come and get you in an hour."

"Okay." Feeling flustered, I bite back a dopey grin and take a sip of my coffee.

"I see you two are getting close," Chef Casey says, coming up beside me for a cup of water.

"What?"

He winks, taking a drink. "I said you two look cozy."

"Oh, we're just... We, uhm..." Why can't I find the right words? I don't want to confirm it outright, but I also don't want to deny it either.

"It's okay, Leah," he assures me, nudging me with his shoulder. "I didn't mean to put you on the spot. I think it's great. Ben just walked out of here without a scowl on his face. In my book, you're a miracle worker."

Laughing, I relax. "Not a scowl. I'll take that as a step in the right direction. But does that earn me a marshmallow?"

"You're damn right, it does. Take one from the tray over on that counter." He points to a full tray to my left.

"Thank you!" Giddy, I grab a fresh marshmallow and bite into it. "Mmm, ohmygod," I mumble all together. It's so freaking good. Like a soft and fluffy cloud. "This is just what I needed as my afternoon pick-me-up."

"Glad I could help." He smiles, getting back to work.

I head back out to the sign-in table and excitedly wait for the next hour to pass by. When Ben finally comes and gets me, we head out, back to where the cocktail competition was last night. This time, though, the booths are set up for food and icewine pairings. It's a smaller, condensed version of the weekend pass, and since I can't go around to the wineries themselves, this gives me the chance to experience what the other places are serving.

I know I shouldn't be drinking when I have to go back to work this afternoon, but I can't pass up a few small samplings.

Ben is right there by my side, making sure I try everything I want, and even makes a little small talk with those who approach him to say hi or ask for a picture. It's a little weird to see the star-struck eyes of those who walk up to him, though, because I just see him as Ben.

I try and step to the side to give him his space and avoid any questions about who I am, but Ben doesn't let me. He reaches out and wraps his arm around me, holding me at his side. I receive a few questionable glances and nods of hello before they go back to looking up at Ben. That's who they care about, anyhow.

"You're being nice," I tell him, nudging his side.

"Someone told me not so long ago that my issue with being in the public eye shouldn't be taken out on my fans."

"She sounds incredibly smart."

"She is. And incredibly beautiful."

I feel my cheeks heat despite the cold, and feeling bold, I add, "Well, she sounds like a keeper."

His eyes melt into two dark pools. "She is," he says, and I feel the meaning behind those two words seep into me, planting themselves in my marrow and spreading quickly.

Tucking me against his side, Ben continues to walk us around the booths until I've had my fill.

"I think we've been away from the winery too long," I

tell him.

"It's in good hands. But you're probably right."

"Thank you for taking me. I would've hated to miss this."

"I like experiencing it through your eyes. I haven't participated in any of this in over ten years."

"Sometimes you forget how great something can be because you're so close to it."

"For some things." He squeezes my side and my eyes dart up to his, seeing his face soft and open.

On our way back to Breaker Estates, Ben places his hand on my thigh. "Are you free tonight?"

I love that he thinks I'd have plans. "I am. Did you have something in mind?"

"I want to take you out."

"You do?"

"Yes."

"Okay." Smiling, I turn his hand over and lace our fingers together.

There's no way not to read into him asking me out on an actual date. It makes my heart flutter and my stomach knot in nerves. Nerves from the possibility that this really can be real – him and I. I want it to be so desperately that I fear I'm getting ahead of myself in my mind.

But now…this…I actually let myself feel it, and it feels like I'm floating. I just hope I don't fall on my ass and end up looking like an idiot.

"So, where are you taking me?" Waiting for the rest of the day to pass before I could be alone with Ben again was a slow kind of torture. It's been quite some time since I've been on a date, and while I've been intimate with Ben, going on a date is something else. Going on a date is a declaration of sorts, stating that what's between us is worth taking the time to sit through a meal in a public setting.

"It's a surprise."

"Seriously?"

"Yes, seriously. Why?"

"No reason. But I love surprises."

"Good." Squeezing my hand, he turns the radio on and we drive in a comfortable silence. I see a sign that says we've entered Niagara Falls, and a few minutes later, he pulls up to a restaurant that looks pretty fancy. I glance over at him and then back to the restaurant where a valet is approaching. He opens my door first and then meets Ben around on his side to take his keys.

"I like the lights." I smile, looking at the shrubs and trees lining the front of the restaurant decorated in white fairy lights.

Ben guides me inside, and when he gives the hostess his name, she smiles at the both of us and leads us through the main dining area and out their back doors. I'm confused for a moment, and then I gasp.

"Oh, wow." There are fire pits with people enjoying cocktails around them, but better yet, there are plastic igloo bubbles dotting the entire patio, each one with a table and chairs inside. I've seen these online but never thought I'd get to experience one.

The hostess opens the flap of one of them and waits for Ben to pull my chair out for me and sit before placing the menus down in front of us.

"Thank you." I smile up at her, and when she leaves, I turn my smile on Ben. "This is amazing, Ben. I've always wanted to go to a place that had these."

He gives me a soft smile that has my heart pounding faster. "Good. I thought you might like it."

"I do." Perusing the menu, I find what I want fairly quickly.

The small heater behind our table is keeping us warm and lets me enjoy the snow when it stars to fall. We're literally in our own snow globe.

"Has your aunt contacted you at all while you've been here?" he asks when our dinner plates have been cleared. "Or does she trust you to get it done."

"Oh, she trusts me. But that doesn't mean she hasn't been checking up on me and the status of everything every other day."

"Do you think she'll make you partner one day? Or do you want to start your own company?"

"I don't want to open my own, no. I wouldn't want to compete with my aunt. I always thought I'd just be her second in command, or maybe when I have a few more years under my belt, she'd make me a partner so that she could step back and travel or something." I shrug.

"Would you ever go back to the states so you could be with your family?"

"Uhm," I contemplate, "no, I don't think so. I'm from a small town in upstate New York, and even if I wanted a job near them, there wouldn't be a need for what I do. I would have to move up to Buffalo or Albany, or down into the city or even North Jersey. And if I have to do that, then there's really no point in moving back since I wouldn't be near them."

"Well, that's good."

"It is? Why?" I grin, tilting my head.

"Because," he starts, then pauses, trying to find his words. "Because it is." His nervous smile is so cute.

Does he not want me to go anywhere?

"I'll be right back," I tell him, standing. "I'm going to go to the ladies room."

Ben looks relieved to have the pressure off of him, but I lean down to kiss his cheek so that he knows I appreciate where he was going with that.

When I return, I find Ben has moved his chair to the spot to my right instead of across from me. "Were you lonely over there?" I tease, and his hand comes to rest on my knee.

"Yes," he admits without hesitation, and my eyes dart up to his, surprised at his candor. "I ordered us dessert. I hope that's okay."

"Depends on what you ordered."

"Chocolate lava cake."

"In that case, yes, it's more than fine. That's one of my favorites," I tell him, and he pours more wine into my glass. I take a sip straight away, needing it to steady my nerves. Something about this moment feels big and I'm in uncharted waters, unsure how to navigate.

Luckily the waiter comes in with our dessert, breaking the tense nerves knotting me up. But when he leaves, closing the flap behind him, the air pulses with the same tension I wish I could understand.

"Leah," Ben says softly, sliding his hand up and down my thigh, gaining my attention.

"Hmm?" I hum, not trusting my voice and not knowing why.

"What's going on inside that beautiful head of yours?"

I clear the lump from my throat. "Nothing."

He squeezes my leg. "Talk to me."

"It's nothing. I don't know. I think the wine is going to my head." I try my best to play it off because I really don't know what I would say to him.

How could I possibly explain that I think I'm falling in love with him? It's our first date.

I thought I was in love with my ex, but I wasn't. Not in the least. I've never felt what I'm feeling, which is why I don't know how to deal with it or how to voice it any other way than *I'm falling in love with you...*

And I'm sure as hell not telling him that.

No way. Nope. No thank you.

I'm not crazy.

But I see everything in his eyes. A whole world that I didn't come here for, didn't expect, and didn't think would ever happen. But it's all right there and I'm scared. I'm scared to fall for this complicated man who I thought was one thing but is the complete opposite. And I'm scared a man like him could never truly love me.

Ben wears a shield for the world, but if he'd let me, I'd love to help him step out from behind that shield to remember that the world on the other side isn't always such a bad place. In fact, it's filled with impossibly beautiful things and people who don't care who he is or what's been said about him.

I place my hand over his to reassure him. "I'm fine. I just got a little lost in my head for a moment."

His eyes turn speculative, roaming over my face to see if he can catch any hint of what I'm talking about, but I reach for my fork with a shaky hand before he can find anything.

I slice into the cake and chocolate spills from the center like a dam breaking. But before I can even try any, Ben dips his finger in the liquid chocolate and brings it to my mouth, swiping it across my lips. My tongue pokes out to lick it away, but he gives me a stern shake of his head.

"That's for me," he says, the gravelly tone of his voice making me squirm.

Ben reaches beneath the seat of my chair and drags it closer to him, the scraping of the legs on the cement like a straight shot to my core.

Leaning forward, it feels like an eternity before his mouth is close to mine. And when his tongue slides against my lips, he hums, making sure he captures all of the chocolate before pressing his lips to mine.

Holy shit.

I'm dizzy.

Sliding my hand into his hair, I grip the ends and he

groans into me, making my lips vibrate to the pulse I feel thrumming through me.

Before our kiss gets too out of control and I beg him to take me right here on the table, I cup his cheek and pull back.

Ben licks his lips. "You're my new favorite dessert. If we were alone, I'd spread the chocolate all over you so I could lick it off. There wouldn't be a spot untouched by my mouth."

My breaths come quick and I scratch my nails against his stubble, loving the rough feel of it. It grounds me.

"I wish we were alone," I whisper, "because I would do the same to you."

Groaning, he gives me a hard, quick kiss and then leans back in his chair. "I'll be right back," he declares, standing and leaving the igloo.

I heave a heavy sigh and shove a forkful of cake in my mouth. The chocolate soothes me and melts on my tongue the way I wish Ben would.

Oh, Lord.

I take another bite and wash it down with a few gulps of wine. He returns relatively quickly with a paper bag and holds his hand out for me to take.

I place mine in his and stand, letting him lead me around the patio and through the restaurant. I don't notice anyone or anything else besides him, and when we exit to the street, his truck is already waiting for us.

"I have one more place to take you before I can finish what I started," he tells me, and I look over at him to see the determined set of his jaw and tight grip on the steering wheel.

His desire for me is something that I want to doubt because, I mean, look at him. He can have anyone he wants. But I have no reason to doubt him. He hasn't given me one.

The way he looks at me, like a dessert he wants to devour. The way he touches me, like he wants to make sure I remember his touch. The way he kisses me, like he's addicted to my taste. And the way he fucks me, like he wishes he could imprint himself inside of me, ruining me for everyone else.

All of it.

None of it gives me a reason to have doubt, but it still lingers on the outskirts of my mind, trying to find a crack in the almost too-good-to-be-true bubble surrounding me.

Ben parks his truck, and I was so lost in my own thoughts that I didn't even notice where we were going. I look around me now, but still can't tell.

"Where are we?"

"You'll see." Hopping out, he comes and opens my door, taking my hand in his.

When we cross the street, I see where we are and I gasp. A rainbow of lights illuminates Niagara Falls, and it looks magical and almost unreal.

I squeeze his hand and walk a little faster. I've seen the falls in the summer when I've visited my aunt, so as we approach the railing that runs along the entire sidewalk beside the rushing water, I'm surprised to see a thick layer of ice coating everything in sight. The railing, the light posts, the trees. They're all coated in a few inches of ice from the spray of the falls.

It's absolutely beautiful.

We keep walking up the sidewalk, the sound of the rushing water getting louder. "Ben, it's amazing," I breathe, looking up at him when we're right on top of the falls' drop-off. It seems like we shouldn't be allowed to be this close.

Ben wraps his arms around me from behind and I lean over the railing slightly, watching the chunks of ice floating in the water rush over the side and disappear into the water below.

"Just wait another"–he lifts his wrist to check the time–"five minutes, and it'll get even better."

"How?"

"Patience," he murmurs in my ear, his warm breath a drastic contrast to the freezing cold air around us.

Five minutes stretches on to feel like twenty, but it's worth it when the first boom of the fireworks begins. I flinch at the sudden loudness and Ben tightens his arms around me. I lean back against him, smiling up at the sparks of colors bursting against the night sky.

"I love fireworks," I tell Ben, covering his hands on my stomach with my own.

He gives me a kiss below my ear. "I thought you might."

My heart – the driving force of my body – is beating at a pace that makes me think it might give out.

He planned tonight with me in mind, choosing the restaurant and then coming here believing I'd love it. And I do. I wish we could stand here forever, but when the show is over, I twist in his embrace and wrap my arms around his neck.

"Thank you for tonight."

"Tonight's not over, Leah. Far from it."

His words send a shiver down my spine and I press up on my toes while he leans down to meet me halfway in a kiss that warms me from the outside, in. From where our lips meet, heat blooms and spreads to every corner of my being.

"Ben," I pant, tearing my lips from his. "I need you to take me home now."

Growling, he gives me a hard, quick kiss and grabs my hand, practically dragging me back to his truck.

"It would've been faster if you just threw me over your shoulder caveman style." I laugh, closing the passenger door.

"Believe me," he grunts, "I would've if I knew no one would think I'm kidnapping you."

Smiling, I rub my hands together, and seeing this, Ben blasts the heat for me.

"Thank you."

"I need your hands, baby. I can't let them freeze."

My eyes dart to his and I catch his smile before it disappears, making my chest swell. "I need my hands, too."

"True. But I need them more."

"Whatever you say." I smile, rolling my lips between my teeth.

"It is," he says, and my breath hitches.

I know he's right. Because if he asked me to use my hands to take care of him right now, I would. And if he pulled over and asked me to climb into the back and ride him, I would.

The drive is longer back to his house than I would like, and when we finally make it there, I'm about ready to burst.

Ben grabs the paper bag from the back seat and I follow him inside. "What's in the bag?" He finished his dinner, so I don't know what he could've had wrapped up.

"You'll see," he says, placing the bag on the counter and pulling out a white box. Flipping the lid, I peek at what's inside and my blood rushes, my core throbbing.

There are two lava cakes sitting inside, and when I look at Ben, I find his heated eyes watching me.

"I told you what I wanted to do."

I swallow hard, squeezing my thighs together. "You did."

Placing the cakes on a tray, he pops them in the oven and leans against the counter.

"I want you naked. Now."

"Excuse me?" I manage to squeak out from my tight throat.

"Naked. Now. Take everything off and hop up on the counter, Leah."

"Ben," I whisper, my hands fisting inside the pockets of my coat, suddenly burning up.

Pushing off the cabinets, he backs me up to the kitchen island, caging me in. "I told you I wanted to taste the chocolate right from your skin. And I want to do it here, with you spread out on my counter so I can see every inch of you and eat my dessert the way I want. Okay?"

The okay at the end does me in, dissolving my resolve. He makes a demand, but then asks my permission, as if I could even say no to his desire to cover me in chocolate and lick it off.

I give him a small nod and he rewards me with a blinding grin, momentarily stunning me, and I can't move.

"Let me help." He first slides the zipper of my coat down and helps me out of it, tossing it on one of the stools. Next, he unwraps my scarf and pulls off my gloves, tossing them on top of my jacket.

The rest of my clothes follow the same journey, all ending up on top of the next until I'm standing before him completely naked, feeling more exposed than I have with him yet.

He takes a step back and his eyes peruse me from head to toe and back, meeting mine with a heat that would have singed my panties right off if I still had them on.

"You're so fucking beautiful, Leah," he says with a shake of his head, as if he can't believe I'm real.

It balloons my confidence and, once again, I feel it. I never thought that I would find a man who looks at me like this. Like I'm the whole damn snack, meal, second helping, and dessert.

He's not deterred by the extra soft places on me. The cellulite, the dips, swells, and rolls I can never seem to flatten. All of it. He's taking it all in and the heat doesn't diminish in his eyes.

I know my body doesn't define me. It never has. And my self-worth has never been tied to what I see when I look in the mirror. But with the look in Ben's eyes, I think I'll be viewing myself a little differently. A little better.

"I like the way you look at me," I confess softly.

"How do I look at you?"

"Like I'm beautiful despite all of this." I wave my hand down the front of my body. I want him to know I appreciate it, but his brows clash together angrily.

"Who made you believe you were anything short of a fucking goddess?"

I bite my lip. "My ex, he…he told me I was beautiful, but always had a suggestion for how I could make myself look better. I never felt good enough."

"He's a fucking idiot," Ben growls, stepping up to me, one hand cupping my cheek and the other gripping my hip. "He's a little boy. Men want their woman to look like a woman, feel like a woman, and move like a woman. I want to bend you how I want without feeling like I'm going to break you. I want to hold onto you and fuck you hard, knowing you can take it and give it right back. I want my hands to be filled with your tits and ass and be able to watch them bounce. I want your sexy thick thighs wrapped around my head, squeezing me to the point where I'm deaf to everything but the sound of my tongue lapping up your sweet juices and your cries of pleasure."

I think I'm going to pass out.

"You're perfect exactly how you are, Leah. And I'm almost glad your ex was too stupid to know that. Not because he ever made you doubt yourself, but because now I get to be the one to worship you. Now I get to be the one who tastes and fills your sweet pussy. Now I get to be the one who hears your sweet moans for more."

"Ben," I sigh, my body thrumming alive. I'm standing before him naked and my nipples are so tight, he could simply blow on them and I'd come. I'm halfway to coming as it is. I can feel how wet I am from simply rubbing my slick thighs together.

"Let me show you. Let me worship you."

"Please," I breathe, my throat tight.

Ben kisses me long and hard, until the timer on the oven dings. I have a moment to catch my breath when Ben steps back to take out the lava cakes. He places them on the stove and then returns to me, gripping my hips.

"Up," he commands, and I reach back to hold the counter's edge to use as leverage while he hauls me up, my ass slapping onto the marble. I gasp at the sudden coldness, then moan when Ben's hands slide down my legs.

Stepping back, he puts one of the cakes on a plate and places it on the counter beside me. Breaking into it with a spoon, the chocolate flows out like it did at the restaurant, and I squeeze my thighs together.

"Lay back, beautiful. I need access to all of you."

Doing as he says, the cold marble greets my skin, and I can no longer see what Ben's doing from this angle. I can only see his face, and my muscles tighten and coil with anticipation. I jump when he drags two fingers down my inner thigh, leaving a hot trail of chocolate behind.

His eyes meet mine and he winks, licking his lips.

Oh, sweet Lord, this man is going to be the death of me.

I watch as his head slowly lowers, and the moment his tongue touches my inner thigh, I sigh, then moan as he drags it up my leg.

"Mmm," he hums. "I knew it would taste better on

you."

He slides another line of chocolate down my other leg, this time making it begin almost at the apex of my thigh. His warm breath blows across my wet center and I moan, my hips tilting up.

"Not yet, beautiful," he murmurs, then laps up that path of chocolate too.

He swirls a warm circle around my belly button and steps between my spread legs to brace himself on either side of me, licking it off so only his mouth is touching me.

Flashing me a wicked grin, he dips his fingers in the cake and brings them to my breasts, circling each of my nipples. The warmth of the chocolate cools quickly, causing my nipples to stiffen further, and my teeth sink into my lip, groaning at the pain that's morphing into something deliciously good.

He towers over me, the shaggy ends of his hair falling in his face. My hands automatically reach for him, but he grabs them before I can touch him and holds them out to my sides.

He blows cool air across my breasts and I shudder, moaning and wrapping my legs around his hips, needing to touch him in any way possible.

Ben's eyes stay locked on mine as he bends his head. "Keep them open and on me, beautiful," he instructs, and I watch him latch onto my breast, taking my entire nipple into his mouth and sucking hard, his tongue swirling to gather up all the chocolate.

I cry out. It's too much.

My eyes pinch closed and my neck arches back.

He releases my breast, and the cool air hitting his saliva makes me gasp and then moan.

"I said eyes open."

I find a way to do as he says and he dives in on my other nipple, repeating the same process. My hips rock against his, trying to find any relief that I can. But it's not enough.

"Ben," I moan, "please."

He releases one of my wrists to dip his fingers back in the cake and runs them up the front of my throat and over my lips. He follows the trail with his tongue, and when he gets to my lips, I kiss him with everything I have and everything I want him to know without having to say it. I give him without words how much I want him. And when he pulls back, he breaks off a piece of the cake and holds it to my lips. I take it eagerly, sucking on his fingers and swirling my tongue around them.

Ben's jaw clenches as I give him a small taste of what he's been doing to me. He takes a step back, breaking my hold on him to dip into the second lava cake. He holds up his coated finger, smirking.

Swiping his finger against my core, I moan at the contact, but it's quickly gone, replaced by his hot mouth. He makes a long pass through my wet folds, licking up both my desire for him and the chocolate.

He hums into me, the vibrations making my clit throb, and he doesn't stop. As if a man possessed, he gets one taste of me and keeps going. His tongue dances around my bundle of nerves and then presses down hard, making my vision blur.

I let go, my hips grinding against his mouth as I ride the waves of pleasure washing through me.

When I come to again, I look at him with a blissful smile. He's leaning against the counter staring at me, eating a piece of lava cake.

"Leave some for me," I tell him. "I want to taste it on you too."

"Be my guest, beautiful."

Sitting up, Ben helps me down from the island and I lean against the sink across from him, raising my chin. "Your turn. I need a blank canvas."

With a sexy little smirk, Ben undresses for me. His wide chest and broad shoulders are sculpted to perfection, with his arms looking like he can bench press double my weight. When he drops his jeans and boxers, I bite my lip, taking in his strong thighs and his manhood jutting out hard and thick, awaiting my attention.

"Up," I instruct, and he flashes me a grin that lets me know he likes this little role reversal. Reaching back, it doesn't take much effort for him to lift himself up onto the island with how tall he is.

His cock is closer to my eye level now and I lick my lips, which makes his muscles stiffen and his knuckles turn white from gripping the edge of the counter so hard.

I swipe my fingers through the chocolate on the plate and look up at him, giving him a smile as I slide my fingers down his shaft. I place my palms on his thighs and keep my eyes on his as long as I can before I dip my head down and drag my tongue along the chocolate path, purposefully avoiding his swollen head.

Ben groans and I do it again, this time with a trail of chocolate on the underside of his cock. I grip him in one hand and lift him up so I can repeat the process of dragging my tongue up from his base, stopping short of the head again.

A bead of pre-come drips from the tip, glistening in the light, begging for me to lap it up, but I still don't give in.

I can see how tightly wound he is — his muscles hard, his jaw clenched as he restrains himself, his cheekbones sharper than usual. He sucks in a deep breath, his eyes now hooded slits as he watches my every move.

He doesn't say anything, but every time my tongue touches him, he grunts.

I swipe my fingers through the chocolate again, and still wanting to torture him a little more like he did to me, I put a line of chocolate down the center of his chest to his lower abdomen, and put dots on each mound of his abs. His muscles flex and bunch beneath me as I collect my dessert, making me feel the restraint and power he has within him that he's holding back. He lets me have this moment of control.

I plant a kiss in the center of his chest, finding it so incredibly sexy that he can give me this.

I slide chocolate across his bottom lip and lift up on my toes to suck it off. Cradling his face, I kiss him hard.

"It's taking everything I have in me to hold back," he rasps, his voice low and rough — tumbling over me and scraping my insides.

"I know." I smile sweetly, and his eyes fall closed on a sharp intake of breath. I know he's on the verge of losing it, so I dip the tip of my finger in the center of the cake and slide it around the swollen head of his cock.

Ben grunts at my light touch and I blow cool air over him, making him jump in my hand. I like seeing him hold back. I like teasing him to the brink.

Bending at the waist, I finally give in and lick up the beads of come that have leaked out, swirling my tongue around the rim of his mushroomed head, lapping up the chocolate before sucking just the tip into my mouth.

A groan rumbles from his chest and his hand grips the back of my head. Not pushing me down, but rather holding me there.

Opening wide, I take as much of him in my mouth as I can. And because I got him so worked up, it doesn't take much for me to feel him lengthen and harden as I go as deep as I can. He jerks inside of me, his hot spurts of come coating my tongue and throat.

I swallow what he gives me, taking my reward and moaning around him, the mixed of sweet chocolate and his salty come my new favorite dessert.

Releasing him from my mouth, I straighten, and he slides off the counter. Bending at the waist, Ben hoists me up and over his shoulder like I weigh nothing at all and walks straight upstairs to his bathroom. He only sets me down when the shower is on and the water is hot, sliding me down his torso until my feet are back on solid ground.

Ben washes the both of us and then takes me to bed.

I know I'm falling for him.

I already have fallen for him, and I don't know what to do about it. These feelings are too big to even voice, because once they're said, they can't be unsaid. It's like releasing a gas. There's no going back. You can't bottle it back up and pretend you weren't affected.

Ben asked me about my future at my aunt's company, but I don't know if he was asking because he wants me to stay, or...I don't know. I know we'll have to talk about it eventually, but I don't want to think about that right now. I just want to think about how his arm around me feels like a blanket of protection, and as my heavy eyes close, I welcome the bliss of sleep.

Chapter 13

Waking up half-draped on top of Ben's chest, I don't dare open my eyes yet. He's warm and solid beneath me and I listen to his heartbeat, strong and steady.

He's real.

My legs are tangled with his, and as my breathing changes, he must realize I'm awake because he rolls me onto my back, pressing his entire body against mine.

Without a word, I open for him and he kisses me deep into the pillows, not caring in the least that we haven't brushed our teeth.

His hard length is pressed against my stomach and I tilt my hips up, giving him a silent invitation. Aligning himself at my entrance, Ben sheaths himself in my heat and we move together, instinctively knowing what the other one needs.

This isn't fucking.

This isn't pent-up desperation and need.

This is a comfort. This is different.

This is making love.

He fills me and stretches me, and makes me feel every inch of him as he moves inside of me, building to something greater than what we've already shared.

Ben tears his lips away and presses his forehead to mine, both of us panting into the other.

"Come for me, Leah," he asks of me, his raspy morning voice the last piece of the puzzle. My inner muscles flutter, my legs shake, and I let go.

Sliding my hands to the back of his head, I pull him back down to my lips, kissing him while I fall apart.

He pumps through my orgasm and then joins me with a low groan, stilling inside of me.

I want this with him.

I want this to make it past next weekend.

I want to wake up with him like this every day.

Ben cradles my face and gives me another slow kiss that I feel all the way to my toes.

"Do we have to go to work today?" he asks between kisses.

Laughing lightly, my nails scratch his scalp, loving the feel of his hair falling through my fingers. "Yes, we do."

"Fine," he sighs. "Let's go shower together."

"You make it sound like a chore."

"Not at all." He smirks. "I'm all about conserving

water."

"Of course." I grin. "You want to conserve water."

Conserving water kind of went out the window when I saw the water dripping from his body and he decided to pay extra attention to my boobs when washing me.

✳ ✳ ✳ ✳

Ben drives me back to the inn so I can change and finish getting ready, and then we head to Breaker Estates together. It's sweet of him, considering he only lives down the street from the winery, and has to drive all the way into town for me and then back out to the winery.

Parking his truck out front, Ben turns my face to his and gives me a kiss that leaves me wanting more.

"What was that for?"

"To last me until lunch."

"Oh, okay." I smile wistfully.

Walking in the front entrance together, we both head into the kitchen to grab a cup of coffee and find Charlie, Kate, and Chef Casey huddled together, their faces pinched with worry.

"Is something wrong?" I ask them, nervous that they're about to tell me of a disaster I have to work around today.

"No," Charlie says quickly. "I just have to talk to Ben about an order."

"Sure," Ben answers, his face displaying the same skepticism as mine. I watch them walk off together and I get a weird feeling.

I turn to Chef Casey and Kate, and they look away, Chef busying himself with mixing something and Kate walking over to the coffee maker.

"What's wrong?" I ask Chef, and his eyes dart up to mine and then back to the bowl.

"Nothing for you to worry about, Leah."

"Why do I feel like I'm being lied to?"

"I'm not sure." He shrugs, then gives me one of his flirty smiles. "Don't worry so much."

"Kate?"

She looks guilty. "Like he said, nothing to worry about."

I know they're hiding something, but I choose not to let it ruin the high I'm still riding. "If you say so."

Chef Casey winks, and if I wasn't already completely gone over Ben, I would find his charming ways hard to resist. "I do."

Smiling, I shake my head, stealing a marshmallow on my way out of the kitchen for a little sugar rush.

❋ ❋ ❋ ❋

The day has dragged on and I haven't seen Ben once since this morning. I thought we were going to have lunch together, but I went to his office and he wasn't there.

I asked Charlie if he knew where he was, and all he said was that Ben had to run an errand and would be back later. So instead of a lunchtime quickie, I replay these past few days in my mind, getting giddy at the prospect of another night with him.

I mean, who was I kidding thinking I could keep things professional between us?

At the end of the day, I find Charlie amongst the stills. "Is Ben up there?" I ask, nodding up the stairs to where his office is.

He scratches the back of his head. "Yeah, he is, but I don't know if now is a good time. He's in a mood."

"When isn't he?" I counter, and he offers me a weak smile. "I can handle him."

"Leah, I..." he starts, then stops, rolling his lips between his teeth, holding back from saying more.

"Yes?"

Huffing out a breath, Charlie rubs his jaw and shakes his head. "Nothing. Have a good night, okay?"

"Sure, thanks. You too." I walk away confused, now knowing for sure that something is up.

Climbing the stairs to Ben's office, I knock on his door. "Hey, it's me."

"Come in," I hear him say, his tone clipped, reminding me of the first day we met.

I can think of a few ways to cheer him up, though. "I just finished up downstairs. Do you still have more work to do?"

Ben looks up at me from his computer screen and his eyes are distant, holding a look that I don't understand.

"What's wrong?" He rubs his hands down his face and through his hair, making me nervous. "Did something happen? Is it your family?"

"No," he answers. "But I have a lot to do tonight. Some

unexpected paperwork. You should just go back to the inn tonight."

"Okay," I say, my disappointment evident. "I'll see you tomorrow maybe?"

"No." He scratches the back of his head. "This is going to take a while. Probably a few days. Maybe more."

"You have paperwork that's going to take you days to complete?" I ask skeptically.

I can see the shields he was wearing when I first met him start to rise, and my skin prickles with thoughts of him taking back everything that's happened between us.

"Yes, Leah," he says, annoyed. "I do own this place. I run it. There's paperwork and I'm busy. I can't always be available."

"You don't need to speak to me like that," I fire back. "I thought we were past this. What's really going on?"

"Jesus Christ, Leah," he sighs. "I can't do this with you. I can't. It's too much."

"Are you serious?" Tears threaten to form, but my shock keeps them at bay. "What's too much? You were fine this weekend. We were having fun. Last night..." I trail off, believing what passed between us speaks for itself. "Did Charlie say something to you?"

"No." That single word hits my chest with the weight of a harsh lie. "I just have work to do."

"Fine," I huff, and walk right out of his office, slamming the door behind me.

The tears that threatened to form before now escape my eyes and I quickly swipe them away. I refuse to cry here.

I make a quick exit through an employee side door of the distillery and hurry to my car. I don't make it to the inn though, before the hot, angry tears start to fall down my cheeks, this time not bothering to swipe them away.

I'm angry that he won't tell me what's going on. I'm angry that he's back to being a gigantic asshole. But most of all, I'm angry for allowing myself to believe that whatever these past few days were was something real. He made me believe everything he said to me.

Shaking my head, I wipe my face with a tissue and blow my nose before hurrying inside the inn, keeping my head down.

I don't have the energy to do anything but to bury myself beneath the covers and hope for a dreamless sleep.

Chapter 14

Groggy, I peel my eyes open to a splitting headache and reach for my purse on the floor, rooting around until I find my little bottle of Tylenol. I shake out a few pills and down them with the water I have on the side table and fall back asleep, only waking again when my phone won't stop ringing.

I have about ten texts and five missed calls from my aunt. What the hell is going on?

All the messages are a mix of *call me now* and *what's going on with you and Ben?*

Why is she asking me that?

Sitting up, I swipe her name on my screen to call her, my hands shaking with nerves.

"Leah," she says, answering on the first ring. "What were

you thinking?"

"What are you talking about?"

"Have you not seen any of the articles? I've had people sending me links all morning."

"Articles?" I choke out, my throat closing.

"Yes," she hisses. "I sent you there to do a job, and that job sure as hell wasn't to get involved with Ben Breaker. That's wildly unprofessional. There are pictures of the both of you all over the internet." I can hear the anger and disappointment in her tone.

"Ohmygod," I whisper in a rush.

"God can't fix this for you, Leah," she scoffs.

My aunt was never very loving, always keeping it professional between us even when we weren't at work. I always looked up to her, but even living together when I was younger didn't warrant me seeing a different side to her. Which is why her cold reaction to this and me right now isn't surprising in the least.

"Other articles from five years ago have resurfaced as well. Did you know about all of that? The other women? How he treats them?"

"Why do you assume those are true?"

"It doesn't matter!" My aunt rarely, if ever, raises her voice, which lends to the gravity of the situation. "You're sleeping with him! They found out who you are and now my company's name is in every article, associating me with this shitstorm," she grinds out. "You've embarrassed yourself and me, and I refuse to let future clients think that this is the kind of company I run. One where my employees go after our high-profile clients. We won't be trusted. We'll be second guessed instead of sought after."

"Aunt Violet," I start, and she interrupts me.

"No. I am *not* your aunt right now. I should fire you right now for this, but I need you to finish the festival. But believe me when I say we'll be discussing your future when you get back to Toronto." She ends the call without letting me get a word in, and my chest constricts.

I've messed up. I've seriously messed up.

I can't believe I've put my entire career on the line. I didn't even think I was, though. I didn't think this would happen.

That's the problem though, isn't it? I didn't think.

At least, I didn't think beyond my need to have Ben and how he made me feel.

I've worked for my career for over ten years. I've sacrificed everything to become who I am. And now it's all going down the drain because I couldn't keep my hands off of Ben.

My breathing becomes erratic as I try and get oxygen to my lungs, but my panic is preventing that.

Scurrying off the bed to grab my laptop, it only takes a simple search for article after article from different tabloids to pop up. There are pictures of us ice skating at the winery, mid-embrace when I tripped and fell into him. Pictures of us at the cocktail competition, dancing and kissing. Pictures of us on Main Street during the tasting with his arm around me. And pictures of us leaving the restaurant Saturday night holding hands.

Seeing pictures of us plastered all over the place is disarming, and tears begin to roll down my cheeks again.

The trash articles from his past are placed alongside the new ones, speculating about me in regards to who I am to him and if I was made to be one of the many in his lineup, or made to be a 'house slave' like his ex said she was.

They talk about how he virtually disappeared these past five years, and the speculation is running wild as to what he's been doing, and with whom.

I read everything, my brain not willing me to look away.

Some of them even have comment sections where people have decided to remark on my looks, weight, and job, saying that he deserves better and that they don't know what he sees in me considering who he's dated in the past.

I'm a strong person, but even so, it's hard to not be affected by their hurtful words. I know they're just words from people who have nothing better to do than sit around and judge other people when their life isn't what they want it to be, but they're voicing all the doubts I refused to.

Fresh tears gather in my eyes and I pinch them closed, rubbing my temples.

Ben has to have seen this. Most of these articles and posts span from yesterday into this morning.

I can't believe him.

He knew and didn't tell me.

That's why everyone was being so weird. They all knew, and no one chose to tell me.

The fact that this happened in no way justifies the way Ben treated me, though. There isn't a justification for that.

He saw all of this and decided to push me away and be an asshole instead of showing me.

He's a damn coward.

I shouldn't be treated like shit just because he's splashed all over the internet again. He should've known this was a possibility. I know he doesn't like being out in public, but he chose to take me out.

My chest hurts with the knowledge of his regret.

Is he embarrassed to have been caught with me? Is that why he pushed me away instead of standing with me?

It was okay to be with me when it was just us, but now that the public knows, is he ashamed of me, thinking he can do better?

Choking on my tears, I slam my laptop closed and push it away. Every fear and doubt I've had but didn't let myself think is barreling down on me, bursting the bubble of bliss that I was stupidly living in.

I spend the entire day in bed, crying and wishing I didn't wish Ben was here to hold me. Feeling vulnerable, I try calling him, but he doesn't answer. He doesn't try and call back and he doesn't text me.

Nothing.

I guess when he said he wanted to worship me, he meant only if no one knew.

I don't leave my room for the next two days, ignoring all calls and texts from my family wanting to know what's going on. I have no doubt my aunt told my mom, trying to find out where she went wrong with me.

If I had any close friends, I'm sure they would be texting me too, but I don't. I've only had my career, my family, and myself. All of my friends from childhood are back in New York and I haven't spoken to them in years. Anyone I met in college was just a class acquaintance. Back in Toronto, I only have my coworkers. And my Aunt Violet hasn't tried to contact me again, which doesn't bode well for my future working with her.

On Thursday, I finally manage to shower and get myself as presentable as possible to go in to do a quick set-up for the last weekend of the festival.

Luckily, I only run into Charlie, and I give him a brief wave of acknowledgment before making a hasty exit. I saw it on his face, though – the pity. I don't want it. I don't want to be seen as some wounded baby deer that people think won't survive because of some internet trolls.

I'm strong.

I'm resilient.

But I have my limits.

Ben still hasn't called, texted, or shown up in person. He simply pushed me away and let me be eaten by the wolves all by myself.

I just need to get through the weekend. Then I can forget any of this ever happened, putting Ben and my job behind me.

The first thing my aunt did when she found out was to think of her company, not me. And while I can understand that, I'm her niece, but she had zero empathy for what I might go through after seeing all of that.

Even if she doesn't fire me, I still don't think I can work with her knowing that at any moment, she might if I do something she doesn't like. All she'd have to do is pull out of her back pocket that I've already embarrassed her and messed up once. That's too much pressure.

Getting ready to face Ben and this weekend, I go with a plaid wool skirt, tights, ankle booties, and a loose sweater that I tuck into the front of my skirt. I curl my hair and do my makeup so I look beautiful, confident, and prepared for whatever I'm about to face, even if I don't exactly *feel* that way.

And it works.

For two days, I've managed to do my job and not cry in the middle of the day when I get 'the look' from some of the people checking in. Not surprising, we have an influx of people with all the new attention, most with their phones in hand, at the ready to catch a glimpse of anything newsworthy.

What the hell is wrong with people?

I even had some lower their voices to tell me that they think I'm beautiful and to not worry about what anyone says. All I could manage for them was a polite smile in response and direct them to take their glass of icewine and marshmallow. I know they had the best of intentions by saying that, but I wish they didn't bring it up at all.

I'm almost through with my last day when Charlie approaches me cautiously as the staff is cleaning the tasting room. "Hey, Leah."

"Hi, Charlie." I can't be mad at him. It wasn't his place to tell me anything, and his loyalty lies with Ben and this place, not me.

"How about a drink to cap off your time here?"

"Oh, uhm…" I tuck my hair behind my ear, unsure until he rounds the bar and pours two glasses, deciding for me.

"Come on. Let's go outside for some fresh air."

"Sure," I agree reluctantly, grabbing my coat and following him out to a bench beside the ice rink.

"I'm sorry you have to leave like this."

"I was always leaving."

"Yes, but you know what I mean. I really enjoyed having you here, Leah. Don't tell anyone this, but way more than Janet." He grins. "Plus, you got Ben out into the world again."

"I don't want to talk about him," I say quickly.

"Sure. Okay." He nods, taking a sip of whiskey.

"I did want to share an idea with you before I go, though. The cocktail competition got me thinking that you should capitalize on the win and host cocktail making classes at the distillery's bar. You could do a quick tour and then make a few drinks per class where each one features a certain whiskey or wine made here. They could change with the seasons too, so people have a reason to do it again. They'll come for a good time and maybe buy the products or stay for a meal."

"That's a win-win."

"Exactly. People are always looking for something fun and different to do."

"I love that idea, Leah."

"Thanks." I give him a small smile and drink my whiskey, letting the alcohol numb my insides.

Feeling a pair of eyes on me, I look past the rink to the windows of The Whiskey Room to find Ben standing there. He pushes the door open to join us and my chest tightens at the sight of him.

Charlie follows my gaze, sighing. "I'll be sure to run the idea by him, but I think it's amazing and want to make it happen. Which means you have to come back for my inaugural class."

"What class?" Ben asks, and I close my eyes at the sound of his voice, holding back tears. It's been a week since I've heard it, and the deep timbre vibrates through me.

Be strong. I've got this.

"I'll tell you about it later," Charlie tells him, and then pulls me in for a hug. "Don't be a stranger."

My throat is clogged with emotions, so all I can manage is a nod, and then he's leaving me alone with Ben.

The air around us is charged with a week's worth of anger, pain, sadness, and regret, but my heart still pounds for the man in front of me.

I don't say anything to him. I swirl the whiskey in my glass and then gulp it down in a single shot, not even wincing at the burn. I need it to remain numb to the conversation we're about to have. I have a feeling I won't want to feel anything in the next few minutes.

"I need to talk to you," he says, making sure to keep a few feet of distance between us.

"You do? Because it's been a week and you haven't had anything to say. But you do now that I'm leaving?"

"Yes," he admits, and my eyes flash up to his.

"I saw everything online, Ben. Is that why you said you couldn't do this anymore?"

"Yes," he confesses again, only making me angrier.

"I had to hear it from my aunt Monday morning when she called to tell me I was sullying her company's name. You should've been the one to tell me, Ben, but you chose to push me away. This entire week, you didn't reach out once. *Not once* to see if I was okay."

Shaking my head, I swipe at a rogue tear that's escaped my eye. Standing, I walk a few feet away and then turn back to him, holding my arms out in defeat. "I guess what happened between us didn't mean as much to you as it did to me. Or maybe you're ashamed to be with me and you realized you made a mistake. I don't know, but..." I trail off, sucking in a shaky breath. I have to look away, not wanting to see the truth in his eyes. Or rather, not *ready* to see the truth in them.

"Leah," he whispers, his voice strained.

"No, Ben. I don't want to hear it. If you didn't feel that way, you wouldn't have sent me away. You would've warned me. You would've been there for me, called me, showed up at some point to check on me. Hell, I would've even taken a text. But you waited until I was leaving to say something. You're a coward, Ben. I don't even care what's being said about me. I don't care what they think about me, you, us — none of it. I don't know those people. They're strangers

194

behind a keyboard. But it's clear you still care about all of that."

"Leah…" he starts again, but then clenches his jaw shut, unable to find anything to say.

"You may think that you've moved on, but all you've done to actually move on from your past is hide, hoping no one would find you so you wouldn't have to deal with what happened five years ago."

"I have dealt with it," he tries to defend, but I cut him off.

"You haven't. It's clear you can't handle this." I motion between the two of us. "And I need a man who can. Especially when things get tough."

"Leah, I didn't mean to ignore you like that, I–"

"Yes, you did, or you wouldn't have done it. You had to have known that taking me out in public would've had the potential to play out the way it did. I did. I'm not her, Ben. I'm not your ex. I'm not going to, and I never was going to, talk to the press about you. I would have nothing positive to gain from that."

"Leah, I fucked up."

"Yes, you did."

"This was real for me, Leah. This *is real* for me." He pounds his fist to his chest. "But seeing us plastered all over the internet…" He shakes his head. "I didn't want that for you. I didn't want you to see what they were saying. I didn't want you to think I'm weak for hating that this was happening to me again and I didn't know what to do."

"I saw anyway, Ben," I say, throwing my hands up. "I'm

very aware of how I look. Those people commenting about me are the ones who wish they could be with you and think tearing me down would get them there. And you know what?" I pause. "Now they have the opportunity. Because I'm taking myself out of the running."

Shaking my head, I place my glass down on the bench harder than necessary. "I can't believe I fell in love with a coward." Ben's eyes widen in surprise. "I think it was just the magic of this place, though, because I can't be with someone, or love someone, who doesn't believe in us or me."

He doesn't say anything. Nothing. He just looks at me with an emotionless expression, like he's shut down and didn't hear a single thing I said.

"So, bye, Ben. I hope you enjoy your life hiding behind these walls." Shoving my hands in my pockets, I walk away from him, and he doesn't stop me.

He doesn't call after me. He doesn't chase after me like in the movies. He does nothing but let me walk away.

My vision is blurry as I drive back to the inn, tears filling my eyes and flowing down my face. I don't want to cry anymore. I don't want to feel like this anymore. Like I've been abandoned and let down. I just want to leave.

I was going to drive back in the morning, but I can't stand being here any longer than necessary. I shove everything back into my bags, not bothering to fold anything neatly, and load up my car.

"Checking out early?" the woman behind the front desk asks.

"Yes. I have to get home."

"I hope you enjoyed your stay here."

I look up at her, thinking she's joking, but see that she's genuine. "Sure, I guess," I lie, knowing she can full-well see that my eyes are red and puffy.

"Well, we enjoyed having you. Come back soon." She beams, and I manage to force a small, courteous smile out of habit from years in the service industry.

I don't stop for anything on the way back but to fill up my car with gas, and it's only when I'm back in my apartment, two hours away from him, that I feel like I can breathe again.

I make a frozen pizza, open a bottle of wine, and curl up on the couch to watch a crime show until I pass out. I can't stand to watch anything else.

I just hope this heaviness in my chest doesn't suffocate me when I'm least expecting it. I don't see it lifting any time soon. I let myself have a taste of something I had no business getting close enough to taste in the first place, and now I have to face the consequences.

Chapter 15

How did everything blow up so quickly?

One day I was the happiest I've ever been and the next I was miserable and heart broken.

I resigned from my job yesterday so my aunt didn't have to fire me. I thought it'd be easier on her, and I was right. She all but sighed in relief when I did so.

Honestly though, I did it because I couldn't take any more talk on how I've ruined what she's built because I decided to get involved with a client. I already live there in my head. I don't need to be berated for it by someone else.

The worst part of it all is that I could handle quitting my job and I could handle the online bullshit if I had Ben. Over such a short time, he became a safe space for me to live in.

Being around him was an awakening, and being in his arms was like coming home.

And for some reason, I thought it would be a good idea to help me get over him faster if I read every article posted so I might grow to hate him somehow. But it backfired in the worst way. It only gave me a front row seat to pictures of Ben and I looking happy, which made me think of all the what-ifs.

Life doesn't run on what-ifs though, and if I don't stop, I'll drive myself crazy. I should be trying to find another job so I don't end up homeless and hungry and showing up on my parent's doorstep with a broken heart and my tail between my legs.

I told Ben hiding isn't the answer, and I know it's pretty hypocritical of me to hide out in my apartment until this all dies down, but I think at least one more day is acceptable.

He called me last night, but I ignored him. He didn't even leave a voicemail. Although I think hearing his voice would've just made me cry again, so I'm almost glad he didn't. Almost.

My fingers itch to return his call, but I stop myself.

Anger, sadness, and regret flood me all over again, and I crawl back into bed, at war with my self-control to stay away from my phone. Especially when I see his name flash on my screen with another call.

I pinch my eyes closed, a single tear leaking out.

For the briefest of time, I was happy. I got a taste of something I never knew existed and I jumped in when I should have only waded in the shallows. Instead, I allowed myself to be swept off by Ben's strong current into deeper waters I didn't know how to tread.

Waking up the next morning, I search for my phone that's lost in the sheets, my heart clenching when I see a voicemail alongside the missed call from Ben last night.

I want to listen to it.

I want to believe there's something he could say that would magically make everything okay and reverse the choices he made, but I don't know if there is.

So, instead of listening to whatever Ben has to say, I turn my phone off and climb out of bed. I let the scalding water of the shower loosen my tense muscles, then dress in leggings and an oversized sweatshirt. I need to get out for a little bit.

It feels good to have the crisp winter air filling my lungs, the rush of oxygen almost enough to make me dizzy. I shove my hands deep into my jacket's pockets, loving the sound of snow crunching under my boots while I walk the few blocks to my favorite café for an Americano and pastry.

I've never taken a day to just do whatever I wanted. I'm usually too tired from working so many long days in a row, and all I can manage is sleeping, eating, and binging the TV shows I missed that week.

So today, I go in and out of shops, take a ride to the top of the CN tower, stop at another café for my afternoon pick-me-up of sugar and caffeine, walk through the Art Gallery of Ontario, and then treat myself to dinner at a cool little pub where I was able to sit in a booth in the back where no one noticed me.

I did receive a few odd looks of confusion when walking about, like they thought they knew me, but didn't know from where, and I just kept on walking with my head held high.

Nothing I've done has stopped me from missing Ben, though. And that's the kicker. I fell in love and lost everything.

I kept my phone off all day, resisting all temptations, but as I stare at my bedroom's ceiling in the dark, my weakness wins out and I turn it back on.

Tapping the voicemail, I hold my breath, the seconds of silence before Ben's voice filters through the speaker feeling like an eternity.

"Leah," he breathes, and I choke out a sob, my heart cracking open at just my name. He sounds as broken as I feel. "I need you, beautiful. I need to talk to you. To see you. Please let me explain. I don't want to do it over the phone. I..." he cuts off, and I hear him inhale a deep breath. "I just need to see you. Please."

Silent tears run down my cheeks and I clutch my phone to my ear, restarting his message.

I hear the pain in his voice and it breaks my heart all over again.

I want to go to him. I want to see him.

And it all comes down to that simple need – to see him.

Which is why I throw the covers off and put on the closest thing to me.

Even if it makes me seem weak, I owe it to myself to see

what he has to say. I still have the choice to believe him or forgive him or to drive right back to Toronto and actually try and move on rather than try and forget. Because I can't forget.

Shrugging on my puffy parka, I toss a scarf around my neck and grab my purse, needing to hurry.

But when I throw open my door, my heart lurches into my throat when I see Ben sitting on the floor beside my door, his head resting against the wall.

His eyes pop open, and those two pools of midnight blue snap up to mine, freezing me where I stand.

Chapter 16

"Ben." I blink, not knowing if I'm imagining him or not. "You're here."

"You didn't return my calls."

"You didn't return my call either," I say right back, but then admit, "I was just on my way to you."

His eyes roam over my face, then drop to see my car keys in my hand. "You were going to drive to me in the middle of the night?"

I give him a small nod. "I just got the courage to listen to your voicemail a few minutes ago. But why are you in my hallway?"

"I didn't want to wake you. I was going to wait until the morning to knock on your door."

"You were going to sit out here all night?" I ask incredulously.

"Of course," he says simply, as if he has nothing better to do than sleep outside of my apartment, and my heart melts just the tiniest of bits.

"Come in," I offer, holding the door open for him.

Having Ben in my apartment makes it seem ten times smaller than it is, and I take off my jacket and scarf before I suffocate.

"Do you want a coffee?"

"Sure." He nods, and I make us each a mug of the strongest I have.

Sitting at my small kitchen table, I stare into the mocha-colored liquid in my mug, avoiding looking at Ben. I can't see the hurt etched into his features without wanting to take it away.

"Leah, I'm sorry," he begins, and I follow his hand as he rubs his jaw. "Leah," he pleas, and I know exactly what he's asking for.

Taking a long sip of coffee, I find the nerve to lift my eyes to his, and it's all right there. Everything I'm feeling is reflected in his eyes, mirroring my own.

"I'm sorry," he says again, and I close my eyes at those two words, feeling them as if they were a caress and not just letters strung together. "I shouldn't have said what I did, and I shouldn't have pushed you away. I should have been honest with you and showed you everything before you saw it on your own. I should've been there for you. I just...I didn't want to see your reaction. I pushed you away before you could push me away. You were right, I am a coward. When it comes to you, I am."

His eyes are pleading with me to understand. "I don't deserve you, Leah. You're too good for me. You don't deserve to have your personal life out there for people to pick apart and judge. You deserve a man who's going to step up and stand by your side even when it's hard. Especially when it's hard. You deserve a man who can take you out without you having to worry about your picture being taken." He shakes his head, running his hands through his hair.

"I don't care about that," I tell him, and his brows come together in confusion. "I don't care about people taking your picture or our picture or what anyone has to say about me. Do I like it? No. But if I was with you, nothing else would matter."

"I'm sorry," he says again, and I huff out a short breath.

"I heard you before. I know you're sorry, Ben, but that doesn't make it all better. Are you ashamed to have been caught with me?" That question tastes like acid in my mouth, but I have to ask it.

"What?" he practically chokes out. "No. Leah, no, of course not." Standing, Ben comes around the table and squats down at my feet, taking my hands in his. "I could never be ashamed to be with the most incredible, beautiful, talented, passionate, and caring woman. I love you, Leah."

Tears gather in my eyes. "I want to believe you..."

"I'll do anything, Leah," he rasps, begging.

"Why did you stay away?" I whisper, needing to know. "How can I believe you when you were able to just leave me alone for over a week. And you let me walk away the other day. You didn't try to say any of this then, and you didn't try and stop me."

"I know."

Pulling my hands from his, I push my chair back and stand, walking a few paces away, then turning back abruptly. "You don't love me, Ben. If you did, then—"

"No," he says harshly, cutting me off. Stalking forward, he backs me up against the wall. "No," he repeats. "You don't get to tell me how I feel. Everything I did and didn't do was because I love you." Brushing his fingers across my cheek, I sigh at his featherlight touch. "I don't know how to love you like you deserve, but I want the chance to try."

"You do?" I ask dumbly, and his lips turn up.

"Yeah, beautiful, I do. I can't promise I won't fuck it all up again, but I can promise you that you will never have to doubt how I feel again because I'm going to make sure you feel loved and beautiful every damn day."

My heart is pounding, ready to burst through my chest and into his. He already had my heart since that first frustrating day. I felt the inexplicable pull then, and I feel it now – tenfold.

"Please give me the chance to be yours, Leah. Give me the chance to love you and be the man you need me to be. The man I *want* to be."

"Ben," I whisper, and he cradles my face in his hands. "I want that more than you could possibly know."

"I do know," he says, stepping closer so he's fully pressed against me. "Because I want you more than you could possibly know. I've never wanted or needed anything as much as I do you. Not being drafted into the NHL, not winning the Stanley Cup, not owning the winery, my house, or cars. None of it matters and it all pales in comparison to being with you. You've made me happier than I've ever been, or knew I could be. You brought light and life back into me when all I did was work. My life is yours now, Leah. I want to make you smile and laugh every day, and fuck you every night until you're screaming my name and your eyes rolls back."

My core clenches and my body begins to shake from nerves. It's all right here in front of me – everything I've always wanted and needed.

"I've been miserable without you, and it's my fault. I didn't want to hear that you regretted getting involved with me, and then as the days went by, it felt like it was too late to fix it. But just say yes, beautiful. Just say yes and I'll make sure you don't regret it," he pleas, begging me.

Without an ounce of doubt inside of me, I slide my hands up his chest and around his neck, pulling him down to me so our lips are only a few inches apart.

"Yes."

And it's that single word that holds everything. Ben growls low, fusing his lips to mine in a kiss so scorching, I fear I might burst into flames.

This kiss is everything. It holds everything.

I thought there wasn't a single thing he could say that would make me forgive him or make what he did better, but I was wrong.

I'm more afraid of *not* being with him than risking my

heart and happiness to be with him.

In a frantic fury, we reach for each other's clothes and somehow manage to get naked and make it to my bed before either of us explodes.

Ben doesn't waste time sliding right inside of me, both of us groaning into our kiss.

Stilling for a moment, he looks into my eyes and runs his hand down my side and outer thigh, gripping me behind my knee and pressing my leg up and out. "I almost lost this," he says, planting a kiss to my chest over my heart and then along my jaw. "I love you, Leah. You're perfect. You take me so perfectly, and I can't wait to spend my life finding every way I can fit inside of you."

God, that sounded so dirty, and I love it.

"Yes," I sigh, arching into him. Gripping his biceps, my nails dig into his hard muscles. "But right now, I need you to move. Show me how you feel."

He grins wickedly, his eyes blazing like two blue flames. "Your wish is my command, baby."

Ben pulls out slowly and I drag my nails down his arms, crying out when slams back inside. I don't know how I thought I could go without this. Ben already ruined me for every other man the first time he entered me.

I'm a strong woman, but I'm weak for him.

And I'm okay with that.

I'm okay with my happiness being tied to someone else. I'm okay with needing someone so badly, they're all I can think about and want.

That's love.

And love isn't weak. Not when you're with that person.

Ben gives me all of him and I do the same, my orgasm building quickly.

I claw at his shoulders. "Ben, please," I beg. "I'm so close. Please."

"I'm almost there," he grinds out. "Wait for me." I hold back as best as I can, fighting the urge to give in. He pumps into me two more times before pinching my nipple and growling out, "Now."

I cry out, and Ben kisses me hard, taking every sound that leaves me for himself. They're all his anyway. He can have everything.

"I love you," he whispers against my lips.

"I love you," I whisper back, and he kisses me softly, tears gathering behind my lids.

I have too many emotions trying to fight for center stage, but the only one that matters stems from those three little words that have me believing in happily ever afters.

Chapter 17

1 year later...

"Ben, no." I smile, laughing lightly. "We have to get to work."

"I'm trying to work, but you keep interrupting me," he murmurs against my neck, kissing his way up to my lips.

I push his chest playfully. "I'm serious. We have to get ready."

"Can I at least shower with you? You know how I love conserving water."

"Oh, I know." I pull his face to mine and kiss him until we're both breathless, and then he carries me to the bathroom, making sure I'm extra clean for the day ahead of us.

It's been a dream of a year, and I can't even believe it's *been* a year since I was sent to Breaker Estates.

Ben's come a long way since then. He no longer hides in his office all day, and instead comes down to talk to people. He even agreed to let me submit a request to host an event for this year's Icewine Festival.

After quitting Violet's Designs, I tried looking for another job, but none of them seemed to fit what I love doing, or seemed right for me. That's when Ben asked me to be Breaker Estates' full-time event coordinator and planner. I told him that it would mean being stuck with me all the time, and all he said was *good*.

And let's just say, I showed him how good being stuck with me can be, right then and there.

I have the ability to do any and everything I want, and have made Breaker Estates the premiere location for all events in the area since taking over. Weddings, dinners, parties – I do it all and I love it all. Ben doesn't try and hinder my creativity or tell me he doesn't want to bring attention or publicity to his name anymore.

"How did you talk me into this?" Ben asks as we make our coffees at work.

"Oh, I think you know exactly how I convinced you." I smirk, and he tugs on the end of my ponytail.

"That's right," he says, leaning down to whisper in my ear, "care to remind me?"

A shiver runs down my spine and I bite my lip. "Maybe at lunch."

"I'm going to hold you to that."

Chef Casey clangs two pots together. "If you two are done, I'd thank you to leave me and my staff to cook without the show."

Laughing, I feel my cheeks heat. "Sorry." I grab my coffee and scurry off to the tasting room to make sure all the tables are set and everything is exactly how I want it.

My request was approved by the director of the festival to host this year's icewine brunch, and I've been pouring my all into ensuring the best possible experience for everyone who bought a ticket. A memo was put out that each year, a different winery would host the brunch to showcase the variety of the area.

I've gone with a rustic chic look, and we'll be serving six small plate courses, each one paired with an icewine from the area. The festival is meant to promote the Niagara-on-the-Lake and Twenty Valley areas as a whole, not just the one hosting the event.

Our icewine will be paired with the dessert course where we'll have three miniature icewine marshmallows with two small cups of melted chocolate, one milk and one dark, that they can dip the marshmallows in.

The marshmallows were such a crowd pleaser last year that they're now on our dessert menu full-time and are available for purchase to enjoy out by the fire pits all year long.

We decided to go back to Ben's mom's lobster bisque as our pairing for the festival though, because I know how much it means to him to have that tradition and link to his parents while still moving forward with making Breaker

Estates his own.

For the brunch, we have a mix of rectangle and round tables covered in white linen, and each place setting has a natural woven fabric charger with a burgundy cloth napkin folded into a fan on top. The floral arrangements are in mason jars to keep with the rustic chic theme, each one filled with baby's breath and ruscus greenery like I had done last year, this time having added white anemones and burgundy ranunculus for depth and color.

I thought I loved my job at my aunt's company, but it pales in comparison to working with Ben. I feel at home here. I've found a place where I'm surrounded by people who love and value me for more than just being good at my job. Ben, Charlie, Kate, Casey, and the entire staff. We're a family.

The look on people's faces throughout brunch makes me incredibly happy.

"All I've heard are good things, Leah," Cindy says to me. "You did an amazing job."

"Thank you."

"I'm glad Ben is spotlighting this place more now that you're here. I always believed we had a hidden gem, and now with you here, we're a sparkly, in-your-face gem."

"I like that description." I smile, and the director of the festival walks up to me.

"Leah, this is our best brunch yet. I'm so glad Ben hired you as his event coordinator. I've loved this place for years, and now it's getting the attention it deserves.

"Thank you, Danielle. That means so much to me."

"And it seems you've won the heart of the owner as

well." She smiles knowingly.

My cheeks heat, still not used to people knowing my business. After the whole debacle with the media last year, Ben and I have received quite a lot of attention when we're together, but neither of us ever addressed the horrible things said. We wouldn't give them the satisfaction. We know the truth and that's all that matters.

"Perhaps."

Smiling, she walks back over to her table as the dessert is served, and I slip into the kitchen for a caffeine fix while they finish up the brunch.

※ ※ ※ ※

"Hey, beautiful, let's go have a drink outside by the fire," Ben suggests, wrapping his arms around me from behind. "I even stole us a couple marshmallows from the kitchen."

"Well then, how can I say no?"

"You would've said no?" he murmurs against my ear, his lips brushing against me.

I lean back into him. "No."

I can feel his smile. "That's what I thought."

Shrugging on our coats, Ben takes my hand in his and we walk out to the patio. There's already a plate of marshmallows and two glasses of red wine waiting for us on a table, and I take a sip of wine, leaning back into the chair.

"This is nice. I needed this after today."

"You did such a good job, Leah. Then again, you always do, so it's not a surprise."

"Thank you." I smile sweetly at him, still amazed that he's mine.

"I'm a lucky man, baby, and I'm grateful that you were sent to me last year. You've saved me in more ways than I ever knew I needed saving."

"Ben…" I say, tears pricking the backs of my eyes.

"You're the best thing in my life and I will work every day to make sure I keep earning the love you give me. You gave me my life back, better than it ever was." Grabbing my hand, he brushes his thumb back and forth across my knuckles. "I love you."

I smile through my watery eyes. "And I love you. But now you're making me cry."

"Sorry, baby. Roast your marshmallow."

A burst of laughter leaves me and I spear a marshmallow on one of the long metal poles resting on the ledge of the fire pit. Holding it over the flames, I'm distracted by the bubbling of the sugar and making sure it doesn't fall into the fire, that I don't notice Ben moving beside me until he clears his throat.

"Leah," he says, and I turn to see him kneeling beside me, holding a small black box.

"Ben, what are you doing?" I ask carefully, hoping I'm not imagining this.

Smiling shyly, he opens the box and I gasp, seeing the most beautiful ring nestled inside the velour padding.

"Ben, what are you doing?" I ask again.

"What does it look like I'm doing? Because to me, it looks like you're interrupting me while I'm trying to ask you the most important question of my life."

"Okay," is all I manage to say, clamping my mouth shut while the tears from before come back with a vengeance, falling silently from my eyes.

"So agreeable." He smirks. "Now, as I was saying... Leah Walker, I love you, and I want to love you for the rest of my life. I want to wake up and go to sleep with you every day, holding you, as my wife."

I choke out a sob, reaching out to cup Ben's cheek. He leans into my touch. "I want to give you the world, beautiful."

"I don't need the world, Ben. Just you."

He gives me a brilliant smile. One that I get to see all the time now, and not on a rare occasion like a year ago. "Will you marry me, Leah?"

I let my eyes roam over his handsome face, taking in every feature to memorize it for years to come. I may be taking too long to answer though, because I see a flicker of doubt in his eyes.

"Don't worry," I say instead of answering him. "I was just memorizing the look on your face so I'll never forget it. I never thought I could be loved the way you love me."

"You don't have to memorize it, baby. I look at you with my whole heart every time. Maybe you aren't looking hard enough," he teases, and I smile through my tears.

"Trust me, I look *very* hard at you."

"I know." He winks. "But do you have an answer for me, baby? It's torturous waiting."

Smiling, I drop the metal pole with the now charcoal brick marshmallow on it and launch myself at Ben, wrapping my arms around his neck and kissing him with every ounce of love I have.

"Yes," I breathe against his lips. "Of course I'll marry you."

He sighs in relief. "Thank you, beautiful." Pulling my arm from around his neck, he slides the ring into place and plants a kiss over it.

I can't believe he wants to marry me. I know he loves me, and I love him more than anything, but to want to bind himself to me for the rest of his life... That's a whole other level of love. That's a commitment and a promise to be there no matter what.

And to know Ben wants that with me...

My heart swells in my chest, every crack filled and every bruise mended by the man holding me.

I never want him to let me go.

 Icewine Marshmallows

Yields: 2 dozen marshmallows

Ingredients:
1 cup icewine
1/2 cup cold water
3 1/4 ounce envelopes gelatin
2 cups sugar
2/3 cup corn syrup
1/4 cup water
1/4 teaspoon salt
1/2 teaspoon vanilla
Confectioners' sugar

Method:
Boil the icewine in a small saucepan for about 10 to 15 minutes, until reduced to a thick syrup. There should be about a 1/4 cup of syrup left.

Pour the 1/2 cup of cold water into the bowl of a stand mixer fitted with a whisk attachment. Sprinkle the gelatin over the water and let it stand for 10 minutes.

Meanwhile, mix the sugar, corn syrup, remaining water, and the icewine syrup. Bring to a boil and cook until the sugar reaches soft-ball stage (240°F).

Turn on the stand mixer to a low setting. Slowly pour in the hot sugar mixture, allowing the sugar to run down the side of the bowl. Add the salt and turn up the mixer to the highest speed. Beat for 12 to 15 minutes, until the mixture is fluffy and soft. It should hold soft peaks. Add the vanilla and beat for a minute longer.

Pour the mixture into a 9 x 9-inch cake pan that has been greased with oil. Using slightly wetted hands, flatten out the marshmallow. Allow to set for at least 2 hours in a cool dry area. (Do not place in the refrigerator.) Once the marshmallow is firm, remove from the pan. Cut into even squares and dust with confectioners' sugar.

 Whiskey & Icewine Cocktail

Ingredients:
1 oz Vidal Icewine (white)
1 oz whiskey
1-2 oz Cabernet Sauvignon (Old World)
soda
1 Strawberry for decoration

Instructions:
If you want to be extra fancy, you can create Cabernet ice cubes instead of just mixing the cocktail:

Mix 50% with 50% Cabernet Sauvignon wine, and fill the mix into the ice tray. Put it into the freezer.
As soon as they're ready, fill the wine-ice cubes into the glass. Depending on their size, you need 1 to 3 of them.
Mix the ice wine and the whiskey in a shaker. Shake properly.
Pour the mix into the glass.
Decorate the glass with the strawberry.

ABOUT THE AUTHOR

Rebecca is a dreamer through and through with permanent wanderlust. She has an endless list of places to go and see, hoping to one day experience the world and all it has to offer.

She's a Jersey girl who dreams of living in a place with freezing cold winters and lots of snow! When she's not writing, you can find her planning her next road trip and drinking copious amounts of coffee (preferably iced!).

Website, blog, shop, and links to all social media:
www.rebeccagannon.com

Follow me on Instagram to stay up-to-date on new releases, sales, teasers, giveaways, and so much more!
@rebeccagannon_author

Made in the USA
Middletown, DE
04 January 2023

18738390R00137